THE MAN WHO LIVED TWICE

By
ROG PHILLIPS

I0541536

ARMCHAIR FICTION
PO Box 4369, Medford, Oregon   97501-0168

ONE BRAIN TO RULE THE WORLD!

It only seemed like a short time that he had been asleep, maybe an hour at most, but when John Cole awoke in the cradle of his suspended animation machine, deep inside a hidden cave, he found that he had been asleep for over 500 years!

And how the world had radically changed! There were no longer countries or cultures as he had known them. In fact, other than a few scattered pockets of resistance, the entire world's populace was ruled and controlled by one massive brain force in which the minds of all people had melded. And this brain force, called "She" by the few remaining Individualists, was determined to destroy the last pockets of true humanity.

FOR A COMPLETE SECOND NOVEL, TURN TO PAGE 111

CAST OF CHARACTERS

JOHN COLE
His suspended animation device landed him right in the middle of a world-wide "mental" war, in which he became a key figure.

RAG
Falling in love wasn't easy for her—even if she could read every thought and memory stored in a man's mind.

GORSH
As one of the leaders of the last bastion of Individualism on Earth, he had been forced, by duty, to kill the thing he loved best.

WIG
He was the most trusted senior member of the Council—but what was the dark secret he concealed from the others?

SHE
"She" was the massive, all-consuming mental force that ruled the entire planet. No human brain could ever be safe from her.

KIN
The weapon he helped devise was the one last hope for the few remaining pockets of independent human life.

JOAN
Her intelligence was obvious, and she was as beautiful as any woman could be—and she was the oracle for a monster!

CHAPTER ONE

SOMETHING had gone wrong. It must have! John Cole frowned his disappointment without opening his eyes. It had been a little too much to hope for, to expect to really happen; yet it had worked on chickens, rabbits, and dogs. There was no reason to expect it not to work on himself, except that it was too much to hope for.

And it had failed. The bitter disappointment formed creases of discouragement in his face. Then he opened his eyes. His fingers groped and found the toggle that would turn on the light. There was an audible snapping sound as the toggle jumped. The small compartment flooded with soft light.

John blinked at the pain the light brought to his eyes. In a moment he could see. He turned his head and looked at the instrument panel, found the date meter. The numerals, 2436, beamed at him whitely.

2436! His body sagged back against the cradle that had held it for almost five hundred years.

"So it did work," he said, his voice sounding strange. A queer smile twisted at his mouth. There was a regret in it for the rash forsaking of his own time for the future. A realization that whatever was to come, the past, the normalcy of his own times, were gone beyond recall.

He knew now that the reason he had thought it hadn't worked was that he had no feeling of passage of time. His impression on waking had been that not more than an hour could have elapsed. Yet, it had been four hundred and eighty-seven years!

In memory John reviewed that day, long ago, when he had plunged the hypo into his arm, then lain down in the specially designed cradle.

The contents of that hypodermic needle had taken seven years for him to isolate. Seven years of research into the problem of why cold-blooded creatures were cold-blooded, and warm-blooded creatures were warm-blooded. After he had found the answers and proved them by making warm-blooded frogs and cold-blooded dogs and, studying the effects of the prolonged stupor warm-blooded animals fell into when their temperature dropped, he had conceived his grand scheme of using it on himself and sleeping for a few hundred years.

He had thought of every angle to the problem. The fact that he was still alive and healthy after so long a time proved that. The cradle had been designed and powered to prevent setting of the joints and atrophy of the circulation. Air, moisture, and food concentrate had been supplied by a perfect, foolproof mechanism.

He had built his sleeping chamber in a cave he had discovered when he was a child.

The power required to operate all the automatic mechanisms had been very little, and had been supplied by a small turbo outfit with special bearings and special blades that would last indefinitely. The waterpower source had been an underground reservoir draining into a spring. The spring had been stopped up and connected to the water turbine, providing a permanent source of waterpower.

Even with all these permanent, foolproof things to ensure a long period of undisturbed sleep, the antidote mechanism had been triggered so that failure of anything would cause it to work and revive him immediately.

He had told no one of his plans so that no one would ever

invade his sanctum or know that the secret of suspended animation existed.

AND NOW... He climbed unsteadily out of the cradle and stood up, hanging onto a support until the first vertigo of movement passed. His skin was sensitive, hairless. He had expected that from the experiments with the dog. Its hair had dropped off in a few months, but had grown in again after it was revived.

His eyes surveyed the square room of concrete covered by metal tile, recalling everything about it. On the outside it had been disguised to seem a part of the cave wall in case the cave were ever entered by some casual discoverer. The only door was barred on the inside.

For a moment terror licked at his mind. Suppose that after all these years the mouth of the cave had fallen in? That was one eventuality for which he hadn't provided. Suppose debris had piled against the outside of the door so it wouldn't open? In that case all he could do would be to go back to sleep and wait until someone excavated and uncovered him.

More to subdue the growing anxiety than from any desire to exert himself, John walked unsteadily over to the door and lifted each of the three bars, leaning them against the wall.

Then he stood back. The door was free now. A push should swing it open. He hesitated, dreading to find out that it wouldn't budge.

A sharp rapping blow made him jump. It was repeated. Voices came excitedly through the door. As John Cole stood there, bewildered, the door opened slowly outward, pulled by unseen hands.

As the thick door cracked open the excited voices died down. John tried to pick out familiar words in what he had heard. The language seemed to be English or some version of it but so changed that little was left except the familiar sound of it.

The crack widened. Hands appeared gripping the edge of the door, pulling. A man's face, clean-shaven, intelligent, came into view. His eyes were quick and alert. There was a blue-steel shape in his hand that probably was a gun of some kind, though strange in design. The gun pointed at John's middle. The knuckle crooked into the hidden trigger whitened, then relaxed.

"Stah!" exclaimed the man. The door stopped opening. Without taking his eyes off John the man talked rapidly, authoritatively. Other faces appeared briefly and withdrew. In the rapid flow of words the sounds *neck, stah,* and *gih* were repeated very often.

John was already trying to decipher the tongue. He surmised that stah was *stop* with a silent *p,* and from the tone and response *neck* must be the 2436 version of *naked,* while *gih* must mean *git,* the old hillbilly expression for *scram or beat it.* The words flowed too rapidly, however, to make sense out of more than isolated, much-repeated ones.

The clothes the man wore were quite ordinary and obviously manufactured, as was his gun. Parts of the gun were obviously mold-stamped plastic. There was lettering visible along the barrel.

The different voices disclosed that there were men, women, and children outside, and that the women and children were being ordered to leave because he was naked.

Every indication pointed to normalcy and the same old human race still living. Everything indicated he could expect a glad reception and world acclaim as soon as he had proved himself. Everything—except the gun still pointed at him and the tense expression on the man's face. And that whitened knuckle. John sensed that this man had killed often—often enough so that the act didn't hold any repugnance for him in itself.

But whatever lay behind those significant signs, he was evidently going to get a hearing instead of a bullet. He forgot about it and smiled at the sounds of disappointed kids being herded out of the cave by excited women.

NOT UNTIL their voices died in the distance did the door open further. Then it was opened swiftly to reveal a ring of armed men, their faces cold and grim.

"Hoor," the leader clipped.

"I take it you're asking me who I am," John said slowly. "I'm John Cole. I've been in here since 1949, in suspended animation."

Another of the hostile ring said clearly, "Trick!" Worried eyes glanced at the leader briefly and back to John. The leader slowly shook his head.

"Ntrick," he said flatly. Then to John, "I've been quite a student of the ancient recordings, and speak old American fluently. I can believe you. However, you must submit to certain tests to prove this isn't a trick. If it is a trick, you must know those tests and know they will reveal you."

"I'm telling the truth," John said, relaxing. "I'm glad you have tests to prove it, because it will set you at ease sooner. Those guns pointed at me tickle my ribs."

A brief smile flickered on the face of the leader, but he didn't answer. A man came into the cave with some clothes under his arm and tossed them at John, who tried to catch them. They hit him and dropped to the floor before he could get his hands up to grasp them. He bent over to pick them up. A vertigo seized him. He started to fall.

Hands caught him and held him up, but a shrill, angry voice screamed, "Undo!" and the hands dropped away. They had prevented the fall, though, and John slowly and carefully pulled on trousers and shirt. The shoes were nothing but soles with straps to hold them on, styled in the pattern of the woman's slipper without any heel. John sat on the dirt floor of the cave while he mastered the problem of putting them on. When he finished he looked up and smiled his thanks.

The leader then turned and went to the entrance of the cave. John watched him and saw the face of a young girl peek in at him, eyes large and round.

The girl talked in a low voice to the man, eagerly and insistently. The man listened, nodding his head gravely from time to time. Finally he turned and came hack, pointing his gun once more at John.

"Now it comes," John muttered.

"You have passed the tests," the man said. After he said it he looked from one to another of his companions, smiling, then dramatically holstered his gun. The others did the same.

The ring of menacing guns changed to a ring of smiling faces. The leader advanced, hand outstretched.

"My name is Gorsh," he said, his smile wide. "You are weak and need food and rest. Otherwise I'd introduce you to the others. I will let Rag meet you, though. If he weren't with us I would have had to kill you. Rag!"

The girl with the large round eyes stepped timidly inside the entrance.

"This is John Cole, Rag," Gorsh said jovially.

Rag stared at John's face fixedly for perhaps five seconds. Suddenly she giggled. Her face turned pink. She turned and ran from the cave in confusion.

John stared after the retreating figure. Rag was gone before he fully realized that Gorsh had distinctly said, "If *he* weren't with us." John turned to Gorsh determinedly.

"Is Rag a boy or a girl?" he asked.

"He's my daughter," Gorsh said quietly. There was a note of quiet pride as he said it. He added, almost as an afterthought, "He's a natural."

CHAPTER TWO

IT WAS a full ten days before John was again able to view his surroundings with any degree of interest after that first half-hour of meeting. He could remember later wondering what had happened to the feminine pronoun in "old American". When Gorsh had proudly announced that "Rag was a natural", his head had been spinning.

After that there had been nightmarish memories of a rough, swaying trip that seemed to last forever. He knew he was being carried.

In a later infinite duration of painful existence he was aware of a hospital room, the doctors and nurses quite normal-looking. Periodically they forced him to eat. Each time he promptly threw up whatever it was he had swallowed. Even water wouldn't stay down.

During that period he had been convinced that he must have caught some bad disease, and that his five centuries of suspended animation and his awakening were delusions.

The climb to the full resumption of all bodily functions was steep all the way. For two days moisture and food had to be introduced intravenously. The stomach refused to hold anything at all.

It might never have retained anything if one of the doctors had not had the happy inspiration of completely anesthetizing the stomach muscles. Intravenous feeding was continued while a neutral gel was fed into the stomach, a pint every hour, until normal process of the stomach and intestines was established.

This procedure was just started by the time the intravenous feeding had begun to make its effects felt. Immediately John was caught up in the problem. It was a necessary adjunct of his own special field of suspended animation, and was necessary to complete his reports. Anyone in the future who wished to suspend animation for any length of time would have to know the procedure for starting life again. The necessary equipment and materials must be near at hand in the sleep chamber so they could be used immediately.

Thus, the incidents following his awakening in the cave, made unreal by the two days of suffering following them, retreated into the background. The technical problem held his attention. The language barrier between him and the nurses and doctors kept his thoughts within himself.

There was nothing to distract his attention. The room had no windows. The walls and ceiling were an uninterrupted pale blue-green. For all he could find out he might be a thousand feet underground or on the hundredth floor of a super-skyscraper in a gigantic city of the future.

The treatment accorded him both amused and irked him. The nurses who fed him his hourly pint of neutral gel, took his temperature, and performed their other duties, wore sterile masks that hid their features. When they talked it was to each other, and in the rapid, senseless end product of good English run riot.

The doctors who dropped in also wore masks and seemed to be working on the theory that he must have nothing distracting like visitors or information about the world to upset him.

AS THE interminably long days passed and his strength returned, he realized that they had probably been right. Intravenous feeding ended and the tasteless neutral gel took on flavor and substance.

John had just begun to wonder if a story he had read once, in which the people of the future had forsaken good natural foods like potatoes and beefsteak for artificial gels and pills, were true when the gel was stopped and he saw his first real indication that the human race hadn't changed much over the years.

It was a cup of coffee, two fried eggs, and some fried potatoes. There was even toast with real butter on it. He enjoyed it to the full. The aroma of the coffee was a perfume of the gods.

After he had finished he had relaxed with the feeling that perhaps now he would be allowed to get up and see something of the world. His hopes were shattered by the nurses and doctors that hovered over him for the next few hours, checking his pulse and temperature. The doctors peered through fluoroscope screens, watching the progress of the food. Wryly John realized that it all must have been doctored with chemicals that would make it show on the X-ray screens, and that giving him a good home-cooked meal had been merely an experiment.

The masked faces and impersonal eyes were so much alike that he stopped being curious about the people behind them. He looked forward to another good meal. When it came he enjoyed it. With sign language he even managed to get an extra cup of coffee.

And during all this time his mind searched out details and pieced them together to form a picture of this world of the future. From the efficiency and expertness of the nurses and the signs of standardization and perfection of every manufactured thing he came in contact with, he built up a picture of a large hospital. The lack of windows and the perpetual masks spoke of carefully sterilized air and controlled circulation of it.

He began to look forward to the day when he would be permitted to get up and see for himself what the world was like now. No doubt Gorsh and his friends had entered the sleep chamber and reported what they found to the authorities, and scientists were going over it carefully.

The scientists would find the exercising cradle he had lain in, the instrument panel with its date meter, and with the date he had started engraved under it.

The story had probably been spread all over the world. When he left the hospital he would probably be given the keys to the city or something, be interviewed by reporters, photographed by newsreel photographers, and deluged with offers of contracts for lecture tours and other things.

No doubt a daily report was released by this hospital on his condition, and millions of people looked for that over their breakfast or listened to it over the radio before going to work.

In these daydreams the time passed more quickly. His years of research were to be rewarded at last. He was to come into his own! And while he dreamed, a few feet away, on the other side of the blue-green wall, her young eyes too full of wisdom, sat Rag, watching him.

IT WAS the tenth day since the stranger who claimed to come from the past and who spoke an old form of American had appeared before Gorsh as he looked into the newly discovered secret cave. Gorsh had just come from talking with the doctor, who had told him that this stranger, John Cole, could now be permitted to get up and do as he chose.

Gorsh silently opened the door to the observation chamber of the hospital room, and stood there for a moment frowning with a mixture of love and worry as he looked at the back of his daughter's head.

Beyond her he could see through the one-way plastic wall into the room where John lay on his hospital bed, apparently asleep. His eyes were kind as he let them rest briefly on the strong chin, regular features, and high forehead of this stranger. There was now a good quarter of an inch of black hair growing out of his scalp, indicating that the five centuries of sleep that had produced the baldness had not destroyed the hair roots.

Gorsh tried to estimate the age of John, then smiled as he realized that what he had been trying to estimate was physical age rather than the actual number of years. This John might have been an old man when he lay down to sleep, and the sleep might have restored his youthful appearance with its slow-healing process.

He dropped his eyes to the back of Rag's head again. His daughter was now nineteen. He had guarded her very carefully all these years since…

She was a natural telepath. The only one in their slowly dwindling community. He, her father, had taught her only to touch on men's minds and never go deep into them. He had realized that when she finally probed to the depths of one man she would fall in love with that man unless he were criminal or base.

He had not wanted her to probe the depths of the mind of John Cole; but he had been overruled by the other members of the council. They had presented the two alternatives: either killing the newcomer at once and taking no chances, or risking Rag's affections in an exhaustive probe.

Gorsh had killed many people, for what he considered good reasons. He could not kill now when there was good evidence that there was no real need. He had given in and permitted Rag to sit here behind the spy wall, watching, probing the silent thoughts that flitted through the conscious mind behind that high forehead.

Not once had they been inconsistent with the evidence. Not once had they even hinted at *contact,* that spectre which hovered over all of them every minute, forcing them to kill, kill, kill. Forcing them to kill even their loved ones—as he, Gorsh, had had to kill Rag's mother almost before Rag had seen the light of day.

The frown on Gorsh's face turned bitter at the memory of that. An had been permitted to live after *it* happened only because of the imminent birth of her child. Her mind had been blanked out, however, and she had been kept in a plain, enclosed room so that she wouldn't know where she was.

The moment Rag had been safely brought into the world, An had been destroyed completely, her ashes spread to the winds, and Gorsh had locked up in his soul all the loving memories of his wife, where no one but he could discover them.

DELAYING An's death until Rag was born had paid off. Rag had proven a natural. Her telepathic gift had survived and developed. More than once it had saved them all by sensing the initial symptoms of *contact* in one of their own number who had wandered away unnoticed and returned unnoticed. More than once it had made possible the acceptance of additions to their number from among the wandering remnants of other isolated groups.

Without her powers of telepathy they would have been forced to kill strangers swiftly.

Gorsh closed the door softly behind him and crossed the small spy room, dropping onto the seat beside Rag. She greeted him with a quick smile.

"The doctor says he can be a free man after today, Rag," Gorsh said in a swift, contracted tongue they customarily used.

"I'm glad, Father," Rag said. She shook her head in amused sympathy. "John's going to have his dreams quite rudely shattered when he finds out how things really are."

"How's that?" Gorsh asked, surprised.

"Having nothing else to do, he's been thinking too much," Rag replied. "He's built up a picture—quite inaccurate in its essential features—about the outside. He's going to be very disappointed when he finds that instead of worldwide acclaim and recognition he has nothing but a precarious future with a small band of fugitives.

"I've been trying to probe his background and discover if he has the ability to understand. I doubt if he will be able to. His twentieth-century concepts may not be adequate for it."

"Well, we'll give him only carefully restricted freedom until we're sure he does," Gorsh said practically. "Any of us would hate to have to shoot him."

Rag nodded, her face sober. "It would break my heart, Dad. Just as yours was broken."

"It would do more than that," Gorsh said dryly. "It would be the end of all of us. Once *She* learned that he had existed and we had killed him, the final drive would begin and there would be no more of us—any of us—anywhere."

"How do you feel, John Cole?"

JOHN OPENED his eyes at the sound of the familiar voice. He hadn't bothered to open them when he heard someone enter, not expecting anything new to happen. He gazed blankly at the visitor during the instant of surprise, then smiled.

"Oh, I feel fine, Gorsh," he said. "Only I'm getting tired of living here doing nothing. I wish you could at least have arranged it so I could have learned modern English."

"Modern English?" Gorsh echoed blankly. "But that's what you speak already, isn't it? At least, that's what the ancient recordings call it." His smile was innocent.

"Okay, have your fun," John said. "You know what I mean. The language everyone speaks around here."

"What was the use, if you were not to live?" Gorsh shrugged. "And now that it seems you will have a chance to live, there is plenty of time to learn it."

"A nice country philosophy," John observed. "But when do I get out of here?"

"Right now," Gorsh answered. "As soon as the nurse brings you some clothes. I'm anxious to show you our towering skyscrapers with their hundreds of stories and," he grinned mockingly, "there are hundreds of reporters waiting at the hospital entrance to take your picture and interview you."

"Hey, give me a little time to get used to things before that," John objected, laughing.

A nurse entered with some clothes. The next few minutes were silent ones as John eagerly dressed. He puzzled over the fact that the clothes were the same type as those worn by the men in the group he had first seen. He had assumed in retrospection that they had been on a picnic or outing of some sort and that back in the city they would wear clothes designed not so much for hard usage as for appearance.

A hasty, furtive glance showed that Gorsh was still wearing the rough clothing, though his guns were missing. He decided then and there that he had a lot ahead of him to learn, and the best way to learn it was to keep his mouth closed and his eyes open.

"There," he said, standing up after fastening his shoe straps. He took several steps, swinging his arms to loosen up. He couldn't remember ever feeling better.

Gorsh led the way to the door. As John stepped through the doorway he halted in amazement. Instead of the hospital hall he had expected to encounter, he found himself in a large natural limestone cave. Memory prodded him. This was a part of the caverns only two miles from the dry granite cave where he had built his sleeping chamber. It had been owned by old man Harper, who earned a small fortune showing tourists through it.

He had been in it several times and knew every inch and

stalactite of it. Fifty feet away across the stream were Winkum and Blinkum, the limestone pillars estimated to be a million years old. This was the middle cavern, two thousand feet from the entrance.

JOHN PIVOTED and looked at the outside of the so-called hospital room in which he had spent ten days. It was a box-like structure of plastic. From the outside it was quite transparent, he saw. Obviously a plastic that passed light only one way, or else the blue-green color on the inside was due to a half-silvering process that gave the same effect. He could see into the room but not out the other side.

There were two lean-tos nestling against the larger structure. One of these burst open now. A boyish figure John recognized as Rag rushed out. She ignored him and talked rapidly to Gorsh. John tried to pick out words, but she talked too fast. When she finished, Gorsh looked up at John.

"So you remember this place," he said.

John stared at him, understanding dawning in his eyes. He turned to look at Rag, who suddenly blushed and seemed torn between a desire to run and a desire to stay.

"I don't need to read *your* mind," John thought. Rag nodded her head, then shook it in utter confusion.

"All right!" John turned to Gorsh determinedly. "The situation isn't funny any more. This isn't a skyscraper and there aren't any reporters and Hollywood scouts. Rag has been watching me brush my teeth for long enough to know me. The fact that you aren't wearing your guns means that you trust me now or else you only have to lift your finger to have me shot by someone else. Tell me what this is all about."

"I was just going to," Gorsh apologized. "What do you want to know first?"

"First," John said, taking a deep breath, "what is the

condition of the world? Are you hiding out from the law, or aren't there enough people to need a law?"

"There aren't many Individuals left," Gorsh said gravely. "We, here, number a hundred and forty-three, including you. We know there must be other small colonies of Individuals scattered in outlying places, but we have no way of contacting them or knowing where they are."

"We live in what you think of as the Cathedral Cavern," Rag volunteered. "It's really quite modern."

CHAPTER THREE

THE CATHEDRAL CAVERN, as John remembered it, had been the most beautiful of the three main caverns. It had been named because of the high shelf at one end where a few dozen evenly-spaced stalactites and stalagmites had met and formed columns similar in appearance to the pipe organ tubes in a cathedral.

There was no longer any possibility of seeing these, however. The entire cavern had been filled in with rooms with plastic walls, ceilings, and floors. Instead of entering a cavern, John and his two guides opened a door and entered a hive of activity.

It was a large, irregular-shaped room. There were dozens of small tables and innumerable metal chairs. At one end was what appeared to be a cafeteria concession doing a brisk business.

At scattered tables were people playing cards. John estimated that every member of the group must be in the one room.

At his entrance every head turned his way. John glanced around with a wry smile, comparing the audience with that he had dreamed of meeting. His gift to the world of suspended animation would be useless with so few to receive it.

Almost half the population consisted of children. Of the rest there seemed no more than a dozen with gray hair. All wore the same blue denim clothing and sandals.

"This is about all of us," Gorsh said to John. "We voted to have a sort of a celebration or party for you in honor of your successful arrival in our time from the remote past. The council wants to accept you into citizenship in our community, and," there was a sly twinkle in Gorsh's eye, "everyone wants to hear you speak. They won't understand you, but they want to hear you."

Rag spoke swiftly to her father.

"Oh yes," Gorsh said gruffly. "You might as well know the main object of this reception. It is to make everyone thoroughly familiar with your appearance and the sound of your voice so that no one will shoot you on sight."

"I don't get it," John said. "You say there are only a hundred and forty-three human beings left in the world so far as you know, including me. Then you imply that if there are any more, and you meet up with them, you'll shoot first and ask questions later."

"Hardly that," Gorsh said blandly. "When we shoot first there can hardly be any questions later, can there?"

Rag took John's arm and tugged at it for him to go with her. She led him toward a close group of several men. John gave up trying to pin down the puzzle plaguing him about these people. There would be time to ask questions later.

IN SPITE of the drab uniformness of clothing, the people all seemed individually to be well dressed. They bore themselves well. The men were tall and muscular. The women were good-looking, and occasionally there was one who was beautiful in John's estimation.

He caught Rag looking at him with stars in her eyes, and discovered that he had been unconsciously comparing the other girls with her and rejecting each one in her favor.

Gorsh was introducing each one by name as the line they had formed moved past. John felt inadequate, as he always had at gatherings where he met so many new faces. He tried to remember the names. Most of them were strange—as names went.

He shook hands with each and repeated that he was glad to know them. They passed on, content with having heard him talk and having seen his face closely.

One little boy shook hands with him gravely and looked up at him. Then he asked, "Aru fithow?"

"Un thew, hund." Gorsh answered for John, and explained, "He thought you were five thousand years old. I explained to him it was hundreds instead of thousands, but I doubt if he knows the difference."

The small group of men who had remained somewhat apart and had not lined up with the rest were finally all that John hadn't met. From their bearing he had surmised they were the council members. The surmise proved correct when Gorsh did introduce them. John classed them as older than himself, and smiled at Rag when he caught the mental trick he was playing on himself. He had gone to sleep nearly five centuries before and slept with no feeling of passage of time. He still considered himself only twenty-five years old.

The leader of the council was an old man who almost exactly resembled Walter Houston as the devil in an old 1940s film, *The Devil and Daniel Webster*. His name was Wig.

Wig's eyes wore a perpetual twinkle. His hard-muscled, wiry body exuded strength. John could see why he was leader of this remnant of humanity. He could have attained a position of leadership in any society.

By the time all the introductions were over John found himself beginning to make a little sense out of the contracted, staccato language. He found himself guessing correctly what was said before Gorsh interpreted it. The council members crowded around him, asking questions about life in the twentieth century. John had almost forgotten that he was completely ignorant of the life of these people when the entrance door opened and a new man came in.

THE NEWCOMER was no different from the others in dress and appearance. It was only his face. His face was working with a strange mixture of horror and appeal.

John heard a gasp beside him. Then Rag's voice burst out in one shrilly screamed sound.

"*She!*"

That sound seemed to be the signal. From a dozen different sources shots sounded, blending into one thunderous roar in the room. The face of the newcomer vanished in a mess of torn, ugly pulp. His body jerked from the impact of slugs as he fell.

John's dazed eyes took this in, then turned to Rag. Rag was standing pathetically alone, the knuckles of her fist in her teeth, her eyes fixed widely on the scene of slaughter. Her face was bloodless.

Now pandemonium broke loose. Dozens of excited voices were shouting. John found himself forgotten as the scattered figures in the room moved into huddled groups. Many were disappearing through a door in the back wall that led further into what had once been Cathedral Cavern.

Six men went up to the fallen newcomer and looked down at him. One knelt and felt for a pulse, unnecessarily. When he stood up the six went through the exit door.

"So they do have a use for the feminine pronoun," John thought. "Or was it the name of that man?"

On impulse he started after the six men who had vanished through the door. As he reached it and went through he heard frantic calls behind him. He ignored them, rushing along the narrow passage that led into the middle cavern.

The sound of several shots ahead spurred him on. He burst out into the middle cavern and then drew hastily back as a slug whistled past his ear. Peeking out more cautiously he saw the six men scattered across the cave, hiding in the protection of limestone pillars.

There were shots coming from the far entrance to the cavern. The sound of these shots was different—more like those from rifles.

The enemy, whoever or whatever they were, were carefully hidden. But there was one figure lying in the open, obviously dead. John tried to make it out in the feeble light of the cave. The cave lighting came from dim bulbs far apart.

One thing was certain. Whether the figure was that of a man or some other creature, it wore clothes different from those worn by anyone John had seen so far—bright red jacket and blue trousers.

Rag was behind John now, trying to get him to go back. Without turning his head he asked, "Isn't that a man out there?"

"Yes and no," Rag said. "Please, John. Come back. You don't know the terrible danger. Please."

He ignored her plea and continued to watch. A figure at the far end of the cavern tried to make a dash for the exit. Several shots sounded. The figure straightened for an instant before toppling. In that moment John saw that it was unmistakably human. The problems he had been puzzling over came to a head. These people who had befriended him and nursed him back to life had lied to him. Not only that, for some insane reason they were killers. They killed all strangers. They killed even one of their own number when Rag screamed the word "She" in a tone of voice that indicated naked horror.

HE HAD to find out what it was all about. How could he find out from people who deliberately lied and said they were the only people left on Earth so far as they knew?

"We can explain it to you," Rag said behind him. "We've wanted to all along, only we haven't had a chance yet. And we haven't lied to you."

"Why can't you leave my mind alone?" John asked bitterly. "Can't I have the privacy of my own thoughts?"

"Yes!" Rag gasped. "Oh, I'm sorry, John. But you

mustn't try to leave. *She* will make *contact,* and then you can't come back. They might even decide to kill you if you won't stay, because you know these caverns. If you were in *contact* we would be found and destroyed."

"What is all this *contact* business?" John asked. "And who is *She?*"

"I can't tell you right away," Rag whispered. "You wouldn't understand. You couldn't."

Part of John's mind had been busy recalling all the things he had known about these caverns. He had known every inch of them. Back of him, before coming to the Cathedral Cavern, there was a small opening off to one side. That opening led into a tortuous passage that led to an exit almost half a mile away.

"Okay," John said suddenly. "Let's go back. But I'm not going to stand for any more mind-reading, understand?"

"I won't, John," Rag said contritely. "I promise."

"All right. You go ahead," John said.

Rag started back through the tunnel with John right behind her. He looked at her slim shoulders, the back of her head with its brown, unruly hair, and doubts assailed him as to the wisdom of what he was going to do. Then he remembered that they had told him there were no more people than those right here. He realized that he had to go out and find out why this small group hid...and killed. He couldn't be sure of finding the truth here. They would probably tell him a story calculated to keep him content, and it might not be true.

The side opening was just ahead now, up a short, steep slope. Rag was even with it. Now she was past it and John was even with it. He took one last regretful look at Rag, then silently ran up the sharp incline. The black hole yawned in front of him. It was a tight squeeze.

In absolute darkness he felt his way, memory alone telling

him which way to turn at each fork in the passage.

JOHN HADN'T realized how much he had missed the sky and the open air until he pushed through the thick mat of bushes that covered the exit. The sky was a light blue with filmy white clouds hovering lazily. The air was a hot breath after the coolness of the caverns, but it was laden with a thousand smells of growing things, and a thousand small sounds made by unseen insects and flitting birds.

He peered back into the opening and saw a flash of light that indicated pursuit. Running at an easy trot he soon lost himself in the trees that had grown up into a sparse forest over what had once been farmland. He didn't stop until he had put a good mile between himself and the pursuit.

Then he sat down on a fallen tree and thought about what he would do next. He had no intention of blithely walking into anything. Even if Rag and her companions had lied, they must have had some reason.

Their fear of that mysterious something they called *She*, and their fear of a mysterious fate they called *contact*, had carried over to him so that he instinctively feared them without knowing what they were. He had to find out what they were, and also find out if there were many more people left on Earth, or whether those men he had seen with the red coats and blue trousers were a wandering band of cutthroats.

The fact that rich farmland had been allowed to go back to the wild indicated a lack of need for the huge quantities of food demanded by a large population. He had just covered over a mile of what five centuries before had been nothing but farms. And today there was not even a house!

John tried to recall what town had been nearby. Small towns used to dot the landscape every few miles. He could recall the names of most of them, and there should have been one almost exactly where he was resting.

He finally decided to march straight ahead, going east, until he struck a road or a house or at least met someone, if there was anyone to meet. He wished now that he had a gun.

Another quarter of a mile and he came across the remains of stone and concrete foundations of houses, regularly laid out. The wood had long since decayed into a peat soil, from which lush weeds reared their heads.

WITH AN abruptness that caught him by surprise, John heard a rushing roar overhead. Startled, he looked up through the trees. The sky looked back innocently.

It had sounded a little like a jet plane, but had lasted no more than two seconds. Still, after five centuries, jet planes, if they still existed, probably flew much faster than sound. Perhaps even a couple of thousand miles per hour.

As his eyes were searching the sky, they caught a movement and settled on it. A fast-moving plane above the clouds. It was in his sight less than two seconds, its silvery shape jumping from behind one cloud to the next. Several seconds after it had vanished another rushing sound drifted down to John's ears.

"So there *are* people!" he exclaimed aloud. "Civilization has gone on along its predicted curve instead of vanishing."

He felt vaguely uncomfortable about it. Now that he was away from Rag and the others, he could see them more clearly. Even though they killed, even though he had seen them literally vie with one another to shoot down one of their own numbers, he couldn't imagine them as ruthless outlaws and killers. He couldn't conceive of Rag being in love with him and still lying to him.

And who or what was *She*? That word might not even be the feminine pronoun any more. It might be a proper name. Or it might be something unnamable.

The plane might have been flown by some being from

another planet! But that didn't ring true either. If that were the case he couldn't see any reason for secrecy. Rag or Gorsh could have told him about that at once instead of stalling on the excuse that he couldn't understand if they did tell him.

A TWIG snapped behind John. The report was like that of a rifle in the hushed semi-forest. He whirled around. A girl stood fifteen feet away, a frown of concern on her face.

She was tall, her short yellow skirt revealed long clean legs tanned a soft brown. Her snug boots of red doeskin were exquisitely ornamented. Above the short skirt was a light-gray coat of feminine design. Underneath the coat was a white blouse.

She wore no hat and John could see that her hair had been set by an expert hairdresser. Its blonde sheen did not come from simple daily combing.

"Well," she said. "Aren't you going to kill me?" She smiled politely at him after her question.

John stared, surprised that she had talked to him in what must be ancient American to her. Did she know about him? Suddenly he realized that her lips hadn't moved when she talked! A crazy thought popped into his mind. Without thinking, he asked, "Are you *She*?"

"Of course!" she answered, her lips immobile. "Isn't it obvious? You are one of the Individuals?"

"I don't know what you mean," John said. "But if you are *She*, you don't look so fearsome to me!"

She smiled absently at him, a puzzled light in her eyes. John's eyes were frankly admiring. He could not remember having ever before seen such a perfect woman. Her face was beautiful without being the character-less beauty that was considered best in 1949. Her form was lithely feminine, with more than a hint of capableness and strength. There was a word for her type of beauty even in 1949: thoroughbred.

"I know about you now," *She* said suddenly, her face clearing. "It's obvious you fell into the hands of the—what we call Individuals. There are quite a few of them in various backward districts such as this. I'm surprised they didn't kill you the moment they saw you."

"Why do they kill like that?" John asked.

"It's a fixation," *She* said. "Civilization progressed, but not all people progressed with it. When the Last Stage was at hand, many balked. Democratic government says that the majority rule, but when the majority decided, these few still refused to abide by the decision. They went their own way. They taught their children that death was preferable to the new way. Their children in turn taught theirs, only by then it had become a holy war to be carried on forever." *She* shrugged sadly.

"I see what Gorsh meant now," John said, surprised revelation in his eyes. "They're what we used to call the die-hards, only they call themselves Individuals. But they mean the same. So they weren't lying. But tell me, what did they mean by *contact?*"

"It's doubtful that you could understand if I explained," *She* said. "It will be much simpler to give you *contact,* and then you will know almost immediately."

She advanced with slow gracefulness. Her clear blue eyes looked into John's invitingly. He thought, "How sane and happy *She* seems. I'm beginning to see that the human race has really advanced a stage in evolution. *She* is as superior to me in every way, as I am to the Neanderthal."

She stopped before him, her eyes only slightly lower than his own. Her hand reached out to touch him. A shot thundered from close at hand.

CHAPTER FOUR

RAG WENT only a few feet after John climbed into the small side tunnel before she missed him. At first she thought he had returned to the middle cavern. She ran back.

Not finding him, she retraced her steps slowly until she came to the place where he had turned off. She saw his footsteps going up the shelf, remembered the small opening. It didn't lead anywhere except into a maze of dead-end bores, so far as she knew. She sat down to wait for him to come back out.

Her active mind reviewed the conversation at the opening to the middle cavern, and the adroit way John had shamed her into stopping her mind reading. He had confessed before to knowing these caverns, and perhaps at one time there was a way out of the caves through that maze. It might be possible that he could break out.

She hesitated between running after him and trying to get him to give up his rash plan to escape, and running for help to go with her and force him to come back. She decided on the former. Wasting no further time she ran up the steep incline and slipped into the black opening.

She had gone only a little way when she heard someone following her. She turned to look back. A flashlight turned into her eyes and blinded her. She gasped, startled and afraid.

"Don't be afraid, Rag." It was the voice of Wig, the chief. "I gather that John Cole is escaping and you are running after him."

"Yes, Wig," Rag said swiftly. "He thinks we have lied to him, and doesn't trust us any more. He's escaping so he can find out things for himself. We've got to stop him before it's too late."

Wig turned the flashlight toward the floor and picked up

John's footprints. He pushed past Rag. She fell in behind him, the two traveling almost at a trot.

They reached the exit seconds after John vanished through the trees. They did not dash out into the open as John had done. Nor, when they found his trail and began to follow, did they rush along carelessly.

While Rag searched for signs of the way John went, Wig kept ever alert, his hands on his guns. No word was spoken. Each was conscious of the danger present about them.

Rag hissed softly when she found traces of someone who had preceded them on John's trail. Wig glanced quickly at the new prints.

From then on, if John had been able to observe them, Rag and Wig showed a skillfulness in being inconspicuous and noiseless that would have amazed him.

They stood breathless, watching, while John looked up and saw the girl. They watched her as she fixed her eyes on John's and advanced toward him. They saw her hand reach into a concealed pocket and withdraw the needle. Then Wig aimed carefully and pressed the trigger.

JOHN'S ATTENTION was snapped back to his surroundings at the sound of the shot. For the first time he became aware that the girl before him was holding something in her right hand. He stared at it dully, his mind going cold at the realization that she held all that was left of what had been a hypodermic needle.

Then Wig stepped into sight around a clump of bushes, followed by Rag. Wig held his gun ready, a cold light in his eyes. He gave John a brief sardonic smile, then turned his eyes to the girl.

"I suppose you wonder why that shot didn't go for your brain," he said coldly. "The reason is I want to have a talk with you, and one unarmed *She* cell, nicely isolated from the others for the moment, is a very good way to do it. Will you agree to a talk? Or should I kill this girl at once?"

The girl studied him for a moment, then nodded her head without speaking.

"This young man," Wig began, "is not exactly one of us. He was born about five hundred years ago, and is here now because he discovered the secret of suspended animation. We've proven that beyond doubt. I can give the details of how we proved it, if you care to hear them; but there are more important matters to discuss."

"Go on," the girl said calmly.

"He doesn't know about you yet," Wig went on. "I doubt if he can even understand what you are. I'm asking you to leave him alone—and us—until we have a chance to present our version of things as they are today."

"I'm sorry," the girl said. "You are members of a small band of backward Individuals who don't fit into modern Civilization. This man, John Cole, is a representative of the civilization of five hundred years ago. We are not going to permit him to remain your captive. His discoveries belong to mankind."

"To mankind, yes," Wig said softly. "But not to *She.*"

"Mankind is *She,*" the girl said quietly. "There was a day when a small handful of Individuals could set themselves up as having more perfect judgement than the majority, and proclaim themselves the so-called saviors of humanity. That is what you are doing, Wig. You can't realize that which you are incapable of really knowing. I who am a cell of *She* should be in a better position to know if being an Individual is better, and I say it isn't. Don't you realize you're like a mother hen who keeps the ducklings she has hatched from going in the water?"

"You...capable of knowing?" Wig echoed. "Even if you disagreed with the majority, as I do, you couldn't do anything about it. There's no antidote for you. No way to become an Individual."

"JUST A MINUTE," John broke in. "I'm sick and tired of all this mystery. I may be from an age before all this began, but I'm certainly able to understand it if you explain it."

"It amounts to this, briefly," Rag said. "You know that I can read your mind, and can stop reading it if I want to. But suppose that I couldn't stop? Suppose that every thought in your mind went into mine at once, and there was no way I could stop it. Suppose you had the same thing. Then every thought originating in my mind instantly went into your mind. Suppose, moreover, that this interchange was so perfect and complete that it would be impossible for either of us to know whether any particular thought originated in either of our minds. And on top of that, suppose the thoughts coordinated themselves so perfectly that we had, in effect, one single mind, utterly incapable of differentiating itself into its two separate component minds.

"Your two eyes each receive impulses, which they make into the mental image. They coordinate so that the mind builds a single three-dimensional image. If your eyes and mine did the same, I could stand on one side of an object and you on the other, and our one mind would get—not a three-dimensional view from one point—but a solid image; something the single mind cannot possibly imagine.

"That's just a small beginning of what *contact* is. Not two individuals becoming one mind, but millions of them becoming one mind.

"This group mind is what is called *She*. It is self-aware. It's an individual entity, just as the aggregate thinking of your own millions of brain cells results in your own mind as a self-aware entity. It's immortal and enduring so long as the cells—the human units—are in any great numbers. Those units can die without changing the greater entity in any real manner.

"Now you have it. You know about as much about it now as you would know about psychology, if all you knew was that the mind is the functioning of the brain."

"With a few slight inaccuracies, you are right," the girl added after Rag had finished. "In the first place you pictured the individual unit as being nothing more than a part of the greater mental entity. That is only partly correct. I have an identity independent of the greater one. I have a name. My name is Joan. I, like you Individuals, have two separate compartments to my mind. One is the conscious and the other is the unconscious. The conscious mind is concerned mainly with the details of my own existence, and ordinarily forms no part of the greater mentality. But I may draw on it at will, and it can draw on me at will. A good analogy is the individual's ability to concentrate attention on, say, a finger, and all the sensations of that finger.

"That is where you Individuals outside *She* have been mistaken. By far the vast majority of the cells of the great mind are almost divorced from it all their lives, except for the benefits they get from it. A man starts to work at something in which he has had no training. He doesn't have to acquire skill by hard study. That skill in the minds of other units is his immediately. Can you play the piano, John? No? If you became part of *She* you could sit down at the piano and play like a master without any lessons. You could know all about music."

"But," Wig cut in, "if you were part of *She* you wouldn't sit down at the piano because you would be doing the bidding of the majority mind, and you would be just a puppet instead of a man of leisure who could sit down at a piano."

"All right," John said. "I gather this much: someone

sometime during the past five hundred years made an important discovery in psychology or biochemistry that made perfect two-way telepathy possible. This discovery created a mind of a higher order than the single human mind. It has certain advantages and certain disadvantages, as all things have. I can see far more of the picture than you think I can. Now I want to ask one question: what produces this thing?"

"It's a drug," Wig answered. "A highly complex selenium compound. No one knows just how it produces the effect it does; but one shot of it, and in a few hours you are part of *She*. That's why we have to kill. If one of our number becomes an integrated part of *She*, he IS *She*, just as surely as your eyes are part of you, John. He can no more follow his own private convictions than your eyes can rebel and look where they wish to."

"And this *She* takes in most of humanity today?" John asked.

"All except maybe thirty thousand rebel Individuals scattered over the globe," Joan answered. "This group headed by Wig will be absorbed within a few days now. I know where they are hiding. The surrounding country is well blanketed to prevent escape. Even now squads should be dropping from planes with the equipment to complete the task."

"ONE THING more," John asked. "The children of the people that make up *She* have to receive the drug before they become a part of it, don't they?"

"They receive the drug when they are ten years old—if they are normal," Joan answered. "If they're subnormal they are kept out and become menial workers. At present there are three hundred million individual menials in the world."

"That many?" John said, surprised. "How many others?"

"*She*," Joan said calmly, "has almost three billion unit

humans."

John formed his lips into a silent whistle.

"Three billion?" he echoed. "And that doesn't include the mental defectives in menial tasks or the children under ten?"

"That's right," Joan admitted.

"And all these three billions form one vast mind known as *She*," John went on, "A SINGLE mind, aware of itself and aware that it is one mind, just as I am one mind and aware of it?"

"Yes," Joan said. "And at this moment most of that vast mind is concentrating its attention through me. Not directly, of course. That would burn my mind instantly. Automatic reflexes prevent that from happening. A unit mind in China at this moment, for example, may be aware of what is going on here only after that information has been relayed through a dozen or more units, each lessening the load on me. There is a maximum of perhaps one hundred minds in contact with mine at any one time, the others being shunted away and seeking other contacts through the ones actually in contact with me."

"All this has developed from the simple discovery of a selenium compound that produces perfect two-way telepathy," John mused, "which makes possible a real, functioning race mind?"

"Not a race mind," Joan said. "The units function together just as the parts of a machine function together, or the cells of your brain function together. The race mind before *She* was a whole only in the logical sense, not in any functional sense."

"I'm beginning to get it," John almost whispered. "I'm beginning to get it."

HIS THOUGHTS were whirling. Wig's eyes were on him, studying him. Rag's mind was touching his lightly, fearful of his displeasure yet stubbornly determined to follow his reactions. Joan's blue eyes watching him reminded him of the one time he had been on a radio program and had been painfully aware of the cold mike being connected to thousands of radios, blaring out every inflection of his voice.

"One thing more," he asked. "Let us suppose I fell in love with you, Joan. You know what love is, don't you?"

"Yes," Joan replied, amused.

"Well suppose I was in love with you and you fell in love with me," John went on doggedly. "Would—would we ever have any privacy? I mean—"

"I know what you mean," Joan interrupted. "Consider the fact that every detail of love is going on at every minute some place. If it is beautiful, there are undoubtedly thousands of units experiencing it through the lovers."

"In other words, no privacy," John persisted.

"Privacy is a concept from the dark ages." Joan said serenely. "It is individualistic and has no place in *She*. You will realize that when you are brought into *contact*."

"Pretty sure of yourself, aren't you?" John asked quietly. He glanced at Rag with a new understanding, and felt a strange thrill as he read her approval of his thoughts. For once he was glad of her ability to read his mind—and withdraw that power when he asked.

"Not sure of myself," Joan replied. "It's impossible to change what is. All one can do is conform and adjust. And you will find that the world has progressed thousands of times faster since *She* was born three hundred years ago than your contemporaries could have dreamed."

"I'm going to shoot her now," Wig said matter-of-factly. "You have the picture. Joan is of no more use, and is a threat while she lives. Do you understand that?" His tone was worried, anxious.

"Wait!" John said. "Don't kill her." He stepped up to

Joan and tapped her carefully on the side of the jaw. She toppled, unconscious.

JOHN WALKED ahead, Joan's unconscious figure in his arms. He felt Rag's eyes on his back, half-suspicious and half-angry. He felt Wig's gun as if it were centered on the small of his back, though actually it was holstered. As his long legs took him in easy strides back the way he had come, he explained to Wig what was in his mind.

"The way you've been fighting this thing you're doomed to failure," he began. "Maybe we'll fail anyway, and mankind will become just the cells of a vast race-brain with no hope of ever ending it. But you've got to listen to my ideas and then maybe we'll stand a chance."

Only silence answered him, so he went on: "I don't know exactly what we can do, but there are two different angles from which to attack this thing. First, there is the matter of quite a few million mental defectives who might be welded into a machine in some way. Also the children and the few scattered tribes of Individuals. Second, I doubt if any serious study of ways of undoing *contact* has ever been made. There may be an antidote."

He walked on in silence for a while, his thoughts active. Another thought occurred to him. "The fact that a selenium compound is what produces two-way telepathy indicates that there might be some radio frequency that could disrupt the thing called *She*. If we could discover that, we could dictate our own terms."

"Radio?" Wig asked. "What's that?"

"You don't know?" John was amazed. "But of course you wouldn't. With all the world one vast mind there would be no need for radio or telephones. If there was anything about radio that affected telepathy in the beginning, I suppose radio was almost immediately banned.

"All we need is time. With Joan captive we have something to work on. Also, we have a definite contact with *She*. Do you have drugs so that you can keep her unconscious indefinitely and bring her out of it when we need her?"

"I think so," Wig said grudgingly. "But if any of that would work, it was probably tried long ago, I think it's hopeless."

"I don't," Rag said firmly. "I believe John's going to find the answer and rescue humanity from *She*."

"How about the siege of the cave?" John's thoughts veered to the more immediate danger.

"That won't last," Wig said calmly. "We've had those before. We kill a few dozen and they leave for a time. They never have discovered the Cathedral Cavern."

"But Joan said they were bringing in reinforcements to really wipe things up this time," John said.

"They've done that before, too—more than once," Wig assured him. "They squirt the first and middle caverns full of the stuff and leave. They don't know we get our air from the other end."

"They would know as soon as Joan recovered consciousness," John pointed out. "It would be a good idea to keep her asleep until we've worked out something where we can definitely use her."

"That's right," Wig said. "And drugs have bad effects on the nerves. We'll have to bring her out of it occasionally or she'll die."

"What I was thinking," John said slowly, "was that I could place her into suspended animation. That way we would be able to forget about her until such time as we needed her. It will take about two days to prepare the shot. Meanwhile, I want a lot of electrical stuff gotten together. I remember quite a bit about the principles of radio, and with the help of a few of your electrically inclined men I can probably rediscover what we need to know to build some sort of weapon."

"Well, we do have quite a bit of stuff that might work for you," Wig said. "Picked it up on raids just like we get most of the stuff we use. You can look it over and decide if it's enough."

CHAPTER FIVE

DURING the days that followed, John found himself fitting into the tribal life of those around him more and more. From the instant of their return from the outside with the unconscious figure of Joan, and their explanation of new plans, a new life seemed to imbue everyone with ambition and purpose.

It took nearly a week to gather the frogs from which the chemical for suspended animation was to be extracted. During that time Joan was kept under drugs. John found to be his delight that there was a large and very adequate laboratory. He spent the time—while frogs were being collected—just examining and familiarizing himself with the equipment of the lab.

Not until Joan was placed in the rocking cradle and the door to the sleeping chamber sealed from the outside, did he turn to the problem of recalling all he knew about radio. He found himself in the role of a teacher, building rudimentary experimental setups and showing highly intelligent men and women the basic principles.

He knew nothing about radar except that it required a crystal to produce the ultra-high radio frequencies. With that meager clue his students forged ahead of him.

He had little to do. He found himself spending a great deal of time with Wig, studying Wig's practical nature that had held the small tribe together and kept them secure. He also found himself spending more and more time with Rag.

There were many things to explore. The record library, composed of wire recordings stolen from museums, told him the story of history from the time he retired to his sleeping chamber until the time he woke up again.

It told him of the first blending of twelve minds in a small farmhouse in northern Wisconsin in 2132. By 2134 the resultant mind had found itself and decided it was superior to anything yet produced.

From then on *She*, as it called itself, embarked on a war of conquest. It was carried on secretly at first. Also slowly. The acquisition of new minds meant their subjugation to the will of the original few. It was found that it took nearly a year for a new acquisition to be thoroughly absorbed and dominated.

John studied these records carefully. He followed through the details of the final conquest of the United States, completed in 2158, giving a hundred and eighty million human minds to the gigantic complex that *She* had become.

In 2165 had come the first international step. Experiment had proved that the telepathic bridge worked without diminution around the world. Missionaries and agents went everywhere, injecting the fatal fluid.

BY THIS time the rest of the world had begun to suspect the evil in their midst. Individual countries began to resist and to wipe out the fifth column among them.

They were doomed to failure. Guns were of no avail against an enemy whose weapon was a hypodermic needle, and whose victories were permanent.

The iron hand of despotism was as nothing compared to the vast mind that took control of even the most innermost thoughts and molded them. A single will was of no avail against the vast will of the increasing millions of "cells," as humans under contact came to be called.

Thirty-five years after the first international step, sixty-eight years after the first birth of *She*, the deed was completed. All mankind except for a few renegade holdout bands in hiding had become one vast intellect, beyond the mental grasp of any single individual. Godlike in its powers and intelligence.

John Cole studied these records and pondered them. He saw that the directives and trends of *She* remained the same as they had been at the start. They had been planted by the first vehicle, and were perhaps the very will and ambition of that first man, Andrew Thorne, who had discovered the selenium compound and stumbled onto its effects.

The death of Andrew Thorne and the other eleven had not even been felt by *She*. It meant no more to that vast mind for one person or a hundred to die, than it would mean to an Individual to forget one little memory. Even less, since all memories duplicated themselves in each human component of the whole, if that person ever drew on the whole and used it.

After 2200, with no more room for expansion, *She* had turned to a stable development of the entire population into one organic whole. Education had been discontinued except for a well-developed plan of indoctrination and basic training in children under ten. At ten their personality was integrated enough to survive *contact*. After that permanent step they had merely to draw on the aggregate learning and skill of the whole for their individual needs.

Wars were a thing of the past. Research spurted ahead as a highly coordinated single task. There was no way of knowing what individuals contributed to it. There was no way of knowing the exact origin of any single idea, since at the instant of its origin it became the property of the whole, and entered the conscious mind and memory of anyone who happened to be thinking along those lines at the moment.

Thus, *She* had come, and expanded until there was no place else to expand. John saw a few of the evils of a dictatorship in it. Life had little value. *She* did not become outraged at the killing of any of the individual units of the whole, as in other times Society had exacted a life for a life. If any individual will balked at personal destruction, that rebellious thought did not outweigh the non-concern of the billions. Thus, as in a dictatorship, quite often the welfare of the individual was subservient to the welfare of the majority and the will of the majority. A majority blended into one single mind!

JOHN COLE, with Rag as his guide and companion, studied the records. He saw the evils of *She*. He also saw the obvious virtues. Rag had been born with the monstrous thing already full grown, its evils exposed, and shown to her to the exclusion of its virtues.

John had been born and grown up in a world where *She* was unknown. A world where nations aligned themselves against nations for destruction, where one race set itself up above others, or one culture set itself up above all others. A world where Utopia was just such a place as the world had now become, where all men were constantly in contact with a greater power than themselves, almost infinitely wise.

He knew of the evils that *She* had wiped out altogether. No longer was one class starved or exploited while a favored few reaped the rich rewards. No longer did one man set himself up and mold history to his capricious whim.

And no longer was it necessary for a man to spend almost a lifetime studying in order to reach the frontiers of his chosen field of research.

It was Godlike! A man who desired music would sit down for the first time to a piano. A power outside him could take his fingers and play them over the keys, bringing out the finest of music for him to hear. A man who desired to know the secrets of all the great mysteries had merely to open his mind to them.

Surely, the thought came to John more and more often, these advantages more than offset the disadvantages. Joan is right. Desire for privacy of thought would merely be a thwarting complex with a person in *contact*.

If it turned out to be possible to destroy *She* completely and return mankind to its former associated but disconnected segments, wars and eternal friction would come once more. Or so it seemed to John. There would be suffering. There would be personal ambitions to be fulfilled at the expense of those less ambitious. There would be national unity at the expense of world unity. There would be class struggle. There would be the tedious and inefficient system of educating each individual so that for a few brief years he could be useful to society before he retired.

ONCE AGAIN the pendulum of indecision would swing. Logic would point out that now society would awaken with the whole world developed into a vast garden. Each nation could start anew with all the advantages the dying *She* left behind.

Twelve generations of universal peace and prosperity would not go overnight. The discipline of *She* would remain to guide mankind. The tradition of *She* would be a binding force that would continue to unite all people into a universal brotherhood.

John would again reach the decision that the greatest right of every man is for individual privacy of thought. The right to love in privacy. The right to the thrill of personal achievement. The right to personal reward. Mankind's destiny was with the Gods, and not on a par with a blood cell, a muscle cell, or a nerve cell.

Joan, in spite of her beauty and personality, in spite of her blue eyes, was little more than a skin cell or nerve end of *She*! And he, John Cole, was a scientist from the past, holding that one nerve ending under opiate while he devised some method of using it to destroy the whole organism! A hundred-and-twenty-pound nerve end of a half-billion-ton, super-intelligent, almost infinitely wise behemoth.

Rag quietly watched the swing of indecision in John's mind. She had learned to do it without letting him know she was doing it. Her mood constantly matched his thoughts, sinking into worried despondency when he was thinking in favor of *She*, rising to elated heights where he swung to a determination to end the monster mind.

She was in love with John. She knew that, unless he did as Wig and Gorsh and the rest expected him to, he would be killed. Never once did she doubt that he could accomplish whatever he set out to do. To her he was not a citizen out of the dark ages. His experiences were too strange, the world of the past that he came from too capable and varied, his knowledge and ability too great for her to doubt that he was more than a match for even *She!*

No one had ever grasped the full thinking power of *She* as John did. She marveled when he detailed in his mind the mental processes of the multi-brain mind, capable of holding all possible alternatives in consciousness and weighing their every implication against the background of a billion past experiences, instantly selecting the best answer.

She marveled at his mental picturing of a world mind with six billion eyes, holding the entire topography of the world in consciousness at one time as a solid thought identical with the actual world.

Rag herself came to know *She* as never before. Doubts rose in her mind as well as in John's. She came to realize that it was something too great for anyone human to grasp. The futility of it grew on her. How could one man, or a small group of men, destroy what was in the minds of three billion people? It was absurd to even entertain the thought!

She began to realize, as did John Cole, that the real vastness of the conscious mind of *She* was not simply an aggregate of billions of individual conscious minds in telepathic contact, but transcended the aggregate, *as the human being transcends a simple aggregate of body cells.*

And an unconscious reverence began to associate itself in her mind with the thought of *She*, that was eventually to change the outcome of John Cole's maturing plans for destroying the monster that sat on the minds of men.

CHAPTER SIX

WIG ONLY half listened to the young man who was enthusiastically describing the workings of the latest short-wave radio that had been built. He was watching Gorsh under veiled lids.

Gorsh, slowly walking toward the door that led outside, presented a picture of innocent idleness. Yet yesterday he had been gone out for over an hour. When he came back he had mud on his shoes, indicating he had gone out of the caverns alone.

Wig watched him now as he paused at the door to look around, and then slowly opened it and slipped through.

"Excuse me, Kin," he said to the young man. He, too, walked idly to the door, slipping out a scant two minutes after Gorsh.

He reached the opening to the central cavern in time to see Gorsh reach the far end. With lithe swiftness he followed, hoping that Gorsh wouldn't pause to look back.

He caught sight of Gorsh often as they progressed through the tunnel to the first cavern, across that to the large opening through which sunlight entered. Gorsh evidently did not expect pursuit.

Before he had gone a mile Wig guessed where he was headed and dropped back out of sight. Now he was more wary of his surroundings than of discovery by Gorsh. He kept his hands near his guns, ready to go into instant action.

He was a hundred yards behind when Gorsh slipped into the small opening to the cave where John Cole's sleeping crypt was hidden.

Silently Wig stole along the base of the hill until he reached that opening. He peered in and saw only blackness. He realized he would have to take the chance that Gorsh was already inside the sleeping chamber. He stepped softly into the cave.

The door to the sleeping crypt was slightly ajar. Wig stole toward it until he could peek in. His eyes glanced only briefly at Gorsh's back before they were drawn hypnotically to the sleeping face of Joan, almost supernatural in its beauty.

As he watched, Joan's eyes opened slowly. Only then did Wig notice the hypodermic needle in Gorsh's fingers. At the sight of Joan awakening, Wig's hands stole to his guns. He did not move, however, but stood motionless, waiting.

Slowly Joan's head turned until she was looking at Gorsh. She smiled sleepily. Then a change began to take place on her face. Wig watched, amazed.

He had known Gorsh's wife, An, very well. As he stood in the darkness of the slightly opened door, watching, he saw Joan's features begin almost to resemble An's. Finally her lips parted.

"Hello, Gorsh darling," she said—only in the clipped speech of 2436 it sounded more like, "Logorshdar."

"An," Gorsh's voice sounded choked with emotion. "I've missed you."

"I've missed you, Gorsh," Joan's voice spoke with the inflections that Wig remembered in An quite vividly. "I've been very lonely, but I've held together, hoping that you would join me."

"I will, An," Gorsh whispered hoarsely. "I would this minute if there were any of the selenium drug within reach. Joan's supply was destroyed when she was captured. The others seem to be steering clear of this area right now."

Wig felt the hair on the back of his neck rising as he listened. It was genuinely An, whom he had seen shot down, whose body had been cremated, whose ashes had been scattered to the winds! Yet she was here, talking through Joan as though she were still alive!

Wig understood now why Gorsh stole away. He as well as the others knew of the store of the sleep drug here and of the antidote. It was simple to administer the antidote in a minimum dose and partially awaken the sleeper, then give her more of the sleep drug afterwards.

Yet, how could Gorsh's dead wife come back to life and speak through Joan? He had to find out, but he could not dare let Gorsh know he had followed him and knew his secret.

As softly as he had come he slipped away, retracing his steps to the limestone caverns. Half an hour later he saw Gorsh slip in and mingle with the rest as if he had never been gone.

WHEN HE knew Gorsh was safely back, he dismissed him from his mind and hunted for John Cole. He found him with the radio technicians, studying the plans for improving the transmitter they were designing.

"Wahntaw, Johnco," he clipped.

John followed him as he led the way to a quiet room where they would not be overheard.

"What is it, Wig?" John asked when they were alone. "I've never seen you with such a troubled expression on your face before. What gives?"

"Is it possible for the dead to talk through the living?" Wig blurted abruptly.

"You have me there," John laughed. "In my day there were large numbers of people who believed in life after death. There were people called mediums who were supposed to go into a light sleep when they talked, or spirits of the dead talked through them."

"It is possible then?" Wig persisted.

"I suppose so," John replied. "There must have been something to it, but I've never had such an experience, I never saw a medium. I never heard a spirit talk."

"I did just now," Wig said. Briefly he told John of what he had just seen.

"Gorsh's wife, An, was in *contact* for a few minutes before she died, wasn't she?" John asked when Wig finished his story.

"Yes," Wig admitted. "But most of the time she was under opiate, totally unconscious."

"So is Joan right now," John said. "What I'm wondering is whether the vast unconscious parts of the mind are also asleep under the various opiates. I can't remember anything of my long sleep. I didn't even have a feeling that time had been passing by, like you do quite often in natural sleep. But is Joan that way? How do we know that *She* isn't very much active in Joan's mind right now while she sleeps? How did she behave when she woke up?"

"She seemed to me to be still half asleep," Wig answered. "Or maybe I just assumed that because she made no effort to escape."

John said thoughtfully, "I wonder if a slight injection of the antidote can be used to just barely restore consciousness. Maybe that's what Gorsh did. Let's ask him."

"I wouldn't advise it," Wig said seriously. "I don't think he should be aware that anyone knows about it. There are some things that it's best to leave alone."

"I guess you're right," John said. "Certainly he knows what he's doing. He realizes that Joan isn't An, and if An tried to escape he would kill her or put her back to sleep again."

John's own words amazed him. In a few short weeks he had unconsciously accepted the code of 2436 A.D., speaking glibly of killing as if it were no more unusual than going to the local grocery store for a dozen eggs. Thinking about that, he realized that he too didn't look on those in *contact* as being entirely human in the same sense that he himself was.

"You think that in some way Gorsh was talking with the spirit of his dead wife?" Wig asked.

"In a way, yes," John answered. "In another way, no. I think that what really happened was this: when An was in *contact* her every thought and memory was gone over by *She*. An was incorporated into *She*, and became a bundle of associated thoughts identical with the original. That bundle was distributed throughout the billions of minds that make up *She*, and continued to have its self-awareness and identity. That's something I'd not thought of.

"I can see what happened now. Gorsh must have divined that possibility and, not telling anyone, revived Joan enough so that he could call into *She* and contact that thought bundle that was identical with his dead wife. She, loving him and seeing the possibility of his eventually being forced into *contact*, had the will to survive. She did survive, though probably the elements of her entire complex are widely distributed. With perfect two-way instantaneous telepathy over any distance that would make little difference. The essential thing is that, however distributed in the physical components, the mental components held together perfectly, held together by the will to survive.

"So An isn't any disembodied spirit of the dead, but actually exists in *She*, and will continue to do so unless she gets tired of the effort. Then parts of her complex will be forgotten by the humans they reside in as memories. Her self-awareness will break up. She will be gone."

"There may really be a true spirit of An somewhere, but if there is, I don't think what Gorsh talks to actually is that spirit."

Wig's eyes lit up with triumph. "I see what you're driving at. You're wondering if perhaps there aren't more such bundles acting like Individuals. You're planning on trying to contact some of them!"

"Yes," John agreed. "The one I want to contact is Andrew Thorne, the man who started all this! I think he was too interested in his creation to ever permit himself to disassociate. I can't deal with *She*, because it is too vast and probably of too high an order to deal with. But I can deal with its creator!"

JOHN COLE stood beside the reclining figure of Joan in the rocking cradle of the machine he himself had built five centuries before. His eyes watched her relaxed face and closed eyes, waiting for the antidote to work. On either side of him stood Wig, the chief of the Individuals, and Rag, the daughter of Gorsh.

Behind them, also watching, were Gorsh and three others. Outside the sleep chamber were several others standing guard. And all of them were waiting tensely. They were waiting to hear the voice of a man who had been dead for nearly three hundred years! A man whose body had long ago returned to the elements, but whose mind, transplanted into other brains, held together by the psychological laws of association even though the various elements of it might be scattered in millions of different living brains, still lived.

Andrew Thorne! The man who created *She!* What would he be like? History said that he had been a biochemist who had specialized in research on organic selenium compounds. History said that he had become famous for synthesizing over one hundred different new selenium compounds.

The record libraries also told in detail how he had discovered the properties of the selenium drug that produced perfect telepathy. He had kept a large number of animals, mostly dogs and rabbits, on which to try out each new drug and observe its effects.

With a selenium proteid, which he called Sepro Nine, he

noticed a remarkable thing. He had been in the habit of feeding the animals all at the same time. He found that among the Sepro Nine animals, when one finished eating, the others also stopped eating, even though they were in different cages and different rooms.

He tried various experiments. In one he isolated a Sepro Nine dog in a room by itself, and whipped it every time he went in. Not only did that dog begin to cringe whenever he entered the room, but also all the other animals that had been injected with Sepro Nine. They all became afraid of him. Their fear of him grew at the same rate as the fear of the brutally treated dog, even though they were treated with great kindness; and no animal not injected with Sepro Nine feared him!

Here he had a proof of some sort of telepathic contact between animals injected with Sepro Nine. He concentrated his research on this single phenomenon. His next step was to obtain a trained dog who knew many tricks and inject him with Sepro Nine. Two weeks after the injection he tried his major experiment.

He now had seven dogs and twenty rabbits injected with Sepro. Only the latest adjunct knew any tricks. Yet when he ordered the trained dog to perform a certain trick, the other seven dogs and the twenty rabbits performed the same trick!

Here was proof positive of perfect telepathic transfer. The educated dog had never once been in the same room with any of the other Sepro Nine animals.

HE THEN invited eleven scientist friends to his laboratory in northern Wisconsin and demonstrated to them what he had done. After that he had published his report in a scientific journal. And that was as far as history recorded the individual achievements of Andrew Thorne.

The subsequent events were known only by hearsay. It

was generally conceded that Andrew Thorne and his eleven fellow scientists had destroyed the Sepro Nine animals and then injected themselves with the drug. What had happened with the first infiltration of the drug? Had *She* come into being at once and dominated Andrew Thorne and his fellow scientists? Had they seen what was taking place and tried to stop it—and failed?

Or had they deliberately created *She* and instilled in it the will for conquest and more conquest? Or—and this was what John Cole thought most likely—had one of those original twelve dominated the others and become *She*?

The answers to these questions could come only by calling up the mind of Andrew Thorne through the *contact* of the sleeping Joan, and asking him. John Cole had spoken to the assembly of the Individuals the evening before, picturing for them what he thought *She* to be. He had explained what he wanted to do, had given it as his own idea, not even hinting that Wig had learned about it by spying on Gorsh when he called up his dead wife An.

Thus, everyone present waited with tense excitement for Joan to open her eyes and for John to call to Andrew Thorne.

John's eyes alternated between Joan and the instrument panel. On that panel was a pointer thermometer with two needles, one registering room temperature and the other the temperature of whoever lay in the rocking cradle. Under suspended animation the two needles stayed together. They both pointed to a temperature of sixty-eight degrees Fahrenheit.

The two needles separated slowly, the body-temperature needle rising. It passed seventy and continued on to seventy-six where it paused.

Joan's eyes opened.

CHAPTER SEVEN

"ANDREW THORNE!" John called sharply. "Where are you? I want to talk to you, Andrew Thorne."

At his words a cloud seemed to pass over Joan's face. It contorted almost imperceptibly in pain. Her eyes opened wider and seemed to grow larger, shining with a light of their own.

An electrical tension made itself felt. John could almost feel a vast presence settle in the room. He felt Rag's hand searching for his and took it protectively, feeling it tremble.

Joan's lips slowly parted, as though with great difficulty. Her throat constricted as if she were trying to speak.

"Who wishes to speak to Andrew Thorne?" The words came slowly, hesitantly.

"Are you Andrew Thorne?" John asked, ignoring the question. His eyes watched Joan anxiously, glancing at the body-temperature needle worriedly. It hovered at seventy-six, twelve degrees below normal body heat.

"I know you now," Joan's voice echoed hollowly. "You are John Cole, who knows the secret of suspended animation." Then, after a full minute, "Andrew Thorne is dead."

"Who are you then?" John asked.

"I am *She*," came the answer.

"But Andrew Thorne can't be dead," John objected. "He would have had the will to live and watch your development, *She*." His eyes again glanced at the body temperature meter.

Joan's head turned with great lassitude until her eyes could see the meter. They studied it silently for a while, then her head turned back so she could again look at John.

"I see what you have done," her voice whispered. "I have

probably underestimated the possibilities inherent in you, John Cole."

"You haven't answered my question," John persisted.

"You have underestimated me, too," Joan's voice spoke. She was silent for several minutes, a smile hovering on her lips. Then she spoke again. "There is a psychological law that eventually brings each individual ego into my central orbit, so that it is One with me, and is no longer an individual. It is the same law that operates in your own mind, John Cole, and in all healthy minds. Its opposite is the breaking up into separate personalities in the schizoid mind, which is the breaking down of the law of Unification. Andrew Thorne had the will to survive and did survive for over a century; but the will needs stimulus to continue, and with the final development of my being to encompass all mankind his curiosity waned. He blended into my being and became One with me."

"Then you are Andrew Thorne?" John asked.

"No," came the answer. "I existed before Andrew Thorne and his discovery of the chemical that produces perfect telepathy."

"How?" John asked, startled.

"THERE HAVE always existed a few individuals among men who were telepathic to a certain extent, so that in each generation there were always many thousands. Speaking in terms you know, the subconscious minds of these individuals were connected telepathically, though not perfectly so, nor constantly so. There was, however, a large enough permanent body of natural telepaths so that I came into being and remained, a self-aware unit whose elements were the subconscious minds of many thousands of human beings. Over the years and centuries they died one by one and were replaced one by one from the next generation, so that my continuity was uninterrupted. Thus, when Andrew Thorne discovered the selenium chemical he did not bring me into existence, but merely tapped my being, for two of the original twelve were already, in their subconscious, a part of me.

"I have used terms you can get meanings from, but I wish to point out to you that those words cannot convey an accurate picture of the reality, and therefore the picture I have given you is only a very rough approximation."

It was John's turn to be silent. His thoughts whirled as they churned over this new facet of the vast intellect speaking through Joan. It had existed even before the discovery of Sepro Nine! The discovery of that chemical had merely opened up to it a positive method of incorporating all mankind into its being!

John tried to picture it by analogy. Suppose he were born paralyzed, so that his mind could only control, say, his eyes? By no act of will could he become aware of his legs or hands. Then a drug is discovered that establishes the neural channels to the rest of his body, and slowly his mind takes them in and is aware through them, controlling them.

In that same way, *She* had been confined to those who were natural telepaths. Try as this vast intellect could, it could not incorporate anyone into its complex who was not susceptible to telepathic impulse. And even with those it was resident in, it had difficulty in controlling. Those individuals were unaware that they were a part of a greater individual of a higher order. Or were they? Could this *She* be the anthropomorphic God?

John shook his head in bewilderment. The thing was too vast for comprehension. Only its basic elements were simple enough to understand. The whole thing rested on two-way telepathy, which seemed to do two separate things. First, it was able to duplicate a mind in other minds and so identify it with the original mind that when that original mind was destroyed by death its duplicate continued in those other minds. Second, a unifying principle created a single ego above the individual ones, just as all the thoughts in a single mind are unified into a single ego called the self.

The first aspect of this phenomenon would account for the belief in immortality. The second would account for the personal God. Yet, if that were so, and there were nothing else, then the so-called spirit world had always been resident in the aggregate of living minds of living people!

John recalled all he knew about so-called mediums who went into trances while spirits of the dead talked through them to their loved ones. Now he could see how those "spirits of the dead" might be actually remnants of the psyches of the dead persons that had crept over into the subconscious of their loved ones, and in the presence of the medium—a more nearly perfect subconscious telepath than the average person—they were able to cross over the telepathic contact established between the medium and the person present, and speak.

He forced himself back to his surroundings. Joan's eyes were watching him, two dreamy pools of blue from whose depths gazed something built on as grand a scale as the sun itself. He felt them drawing him, inviting.

His face was twisted in an agony of desire, fear, and determination as he forced his fingers to inject enough of the sleep drug to kill the antidote and send Joan back into suspended animation.

After he had done it he stood there watching it take effect. And around him the others also watched, while not a sound broke the silence. A memory came to him of a night when he had stood alone on a high cliff overlooking the Pacific, which stretched to the far horizon and to mysterious dark and unguessable depths, and listened to the hushed roar of waves as they emerged from the ocean and broke against the shore.

Joan's eyes closed. The body-temperature needle started its slow journey down to meet its mate, the room-temperature needle. John's eyes turned to meet Rag's. For no reason he kissed her.

CHAPTER EIGHT

AS THE days passed a new spirit seemed to settle over the community in the Cathedral Chamber of the limestone caverns. Lookouts and scouts reported that planes were dropping equipment and men in a large circle whose diameter was several miles and whose center was the caverns. *She* was planning something. Everyone spent idle moments discussing what it might be, and why there wasn't an all-out drive to overwhelm them.

The men who were experimenting with radio worked at fever pitch. They were exploring and abandoning circuit after circuit, going farther and farther into the short-wave bands and into the long-wave bands, and studying each new problem as it came out.

John Cole moved from one activity to another, listening to reports of progress, offering suggestions. It was no longer possible for raiding bands to go out and bring back materials and food. The ring had filled in and tightened so that nothing could pass it. The Individuals were under siege.

A constant guard was kept in the small cave where Joan lay in suspended animation. Wig had decided to do that to prevent Gorsh from stealing there and reviving Joan sufficiently to talk to An. Both Wig and John decided that that would be better than letting him know they knew his secret.

Rag spent most of her time following John around. But she kept a constant watch on her father, worrying as she saw his face grow more haggard each day. She had read Gorsh's secret in John's mind, and now her mental fingers often touched lightly into Gorsh's mind to see his thoughts, and those thoughts gave her grave cause for worry.

Gorsh was torn between duty to his companions and his

desire to join An. He now realized that all he had to do to join An was to escape to the lines of *She* that encircled them and be injected with Sepro Nine and he could then be in *contact,* and he and An could be together again.

Others also seemed to be torn by the same conflicts. More than one person had lost a loved one from *contact.* Everyone now knew that to die an Individual meant extinction, so far as could be known; but that to be in *contact* and then die did not mean actual death, since the mind carried over into the aggregate mass mind and retained its identity after death of the body.

More and more often John encountered small groups talking among themselves. They would become strangely silent and secretive as he approached them. He realized that the seeds of mutiny were sprouting.

They were even growing in his own mind. He found it harder and harder to see the validity of the arguments against the domination of all mankind by *She*. What were those arguments?

They reduced to only one: that every man should have a right to the sanctity of his individual self. Privacy of thought. Only with privacy of thought and the exercise of individual judgement could the individual develop character. Character could not develop where some stronger mind dominated and guided constantly.

BUT DID *She* dominate that much? That was a question that couldn't be answered so easily. Certainly *She* did not permit any individual psyche to become so strong as to dominate large parts of the population and clash with other and similarly strong wills. But, aside from criminal and destructive tendencies, did *She* permit unrestricted individual development of character? And if not, was the desirability of individual development not perhaps an outmoded idea?

Slogans and catch phrases kept recalling themselves to John's mind. "Look to the Higher Power for guidance." "Ask and ye shall receive." And a thousand other expressions taught in the twentieth century and before that. Wasn't the setup now, in 2436, the goal, the ideal toward which humanity had reached throughout its history?

It was that goal except for one thing. Man no longer had a choice. The hypo of Sepro Nine was not held back until the individual asked for it. It was used by force.

Even in the dark ages, when men were forced to accept the Christian faith or die, they could perform lip service while their inner beliefs were inviolate. Before that, when the Romans slaughtered Christians, those Christians could save themselves by disavowing their faith in public while keeping it in private.

The whole thing reduced to one principle: every man should be allowed to make his choice—and to change his mind again after that choice was made.

After John had struggled through to this clarification of ideas, his doubts ended. He had a definite purpose, a definite goal. *She* must be countered with an invincible weapon and brought to heel—or else! *She* was not God, though perhaps closer to that concept than any other thing. If everyone on Earth were killed, *She* would be dead also. If telepathy were ended completely, *She* would be just as surely destroyed, but without harming a single human being!

With his own ideas clarified John spoke to the others. He explained to them what their goal must be and showed them why. He pointed out that if they failed, humanity would be forever dominated by *She*, and therefore the future of the entire human race rested on their shoulders. From then on he noted with gratification that there were no more furtively quiet huddles.

"IT'S FINISHED, Johnco," the young man, Kin, said quietly. John glanced up with a smile.

"At last," he said. "Now we can try the final experiment; revive Joan and bathe her in one frequency after another until we find the one that disrupts the telepathic connection."

"Personally," Kin said, "I think almost any frequency in the short-wave band would do it."

"So do I," John agreed. "But we don't dare risk failure. The moment we try radio waves *She* will know it, and if we don't find the right one at once we'll be bombed out of existence. Don't think for a moment that the instinct for survival isn't strong in that vast mind."

John took a last look at the notes he had been working on, then he rose from his desk and followed Kin in search of Wig.

"We're ready for you to bring Joan over now," John said when he found Wig.

"You are? Good!" Wig grunted. "We won't waste any time then. The latest reports are that the circle has moved closer."

"Get that bank of broadcasters warmed up, Kin," John said. Kin turned toward the direction of the workshop, while John and Wig went toward the assembly hall that opened to the tunnel leading to the middle chamber and outside.

Along the way they picked up others, so that when they emerged into the sunlight there were two dozen of them, all armed with the powerful automatics that seemed to be the only type of gun in existence.

A lookout at the cave entrance reported the circle was still moving in, slowly.

"The scouts over near the cave where Joan is have signaled that the line is less than a mile away from them now," he said.

"We'll have to hurry then," Wig said crisply. "Come on.

Let's go!" He started down the trail at a fast trot, followed by John and the others.

The trees and the rolling hills prevented them from seeing very far in any direction. Each man carried a gun ready as they threw caution to the winds and ran.

Before they reached the cave they heard the first sounds of gunfire.

"Spread out!" Wig ordered. "You stick with me, Johnco."

John followed Wig, a little to one side and behind so as to give him plenty of room for shooting if the necessity arose.

The trees were large, widely spaced, providing good protection if it was needed. The men, spread out thinly so that each could find a separate tree to hide behind, trotted toward the sounds of the shots grimly.

THE GROUND dipped suddenly, then began a constant rise. Visibility through the trees increased. The men who had been posted in the cave could now be seen behind trees, their hands darting around their protection and firing upward in the direction of the top edge of the steep bank in whose face the opening to the cave was hidden.

"They're here already," Wig gritted as he ran forward. "Well, we'll just have to go ahead anyway." He shouted cheerfully, his clear voice carrying ahead to announce his coming.

Tired faces turned at the sound and lighted up with new hope as the desperate men saw the help coming. Quickly the reinforcements took places behind trees where they could command the rim of the hill.

Wig held back, keeping John behind him, until his men had had time to take their places. Then he gave a low call. At that signal, firing began in dead earnest.

"Now," Wig said softly. He darted forward, John following on his heels. There was a brief glimpse of the crest of the hill and of a figure that stood up and aimed at them, then toppled forward with more than one bullet tearing through him. Then the mouth of the cave was just ahead. They were in!

"No time to waste," Wig said urgently. "Pick up your chemicals. I'll carry the girl."

Wig lifted the unconscious form from the rocking cradle and draped it over one shoulder like a sack of wheat. John hesitated as if to argue, then snatched up the small box containing the sleep drug and the antidote.

Wig was ahead of him at the cave mouth, waiting for him. When he came up Wig repeated his signal and the firing started again with renewed fury.

John saw Wig dart forward. A silvery streak flashed down and materialized as a small hypodermic needle imbedded in the nape of Wig's neck. He stumbled and kept on. John caught up with him and jerked the thing out, marveling at the contrivance which was shot at a speed just sufficient to force the needle in, after which the momentum of the plunger forced the fluid out through the needle, emptying the barrel.

Wig came to a stop in the protection of the trees and dropped Joan on the ground. Then he turned haggard eyes to John.

"Quick, Johnco," he said. "Kill me before it takes effect. Otherwise *She* will learn what you plan to do."

A PLAN FLASHED into John's mind. He couldn't kill Wig. He doubted if he could kill anyone. But there was no time to argue. There were others now, ready to do the job unless he did something quickly.

"Turn around, Wig," he said quickly. "I don't want to look at you when I do it."

As Wig turned his back John opened the box and took out a hypo of the sleep drug. Swiftly he plunged it into Wig's back, pushing home the plunger. At the same time he pointed his gun in the air and pulled the trigger.

Wig jerked from the pain of the needle. He turned, thinking he had been shot. He looked into John's eyes tragically, then, as the sleep drug took quick effect, fell forward. He had lost consciousness convinced that he had been shot and was dying, and that was what John wanted him to think, in case the first tentacles of the mind of *She* were already reaching in.

Before Wig reached the ground, ready hands had seized him and were lifting him. Others were picking up Joan. While the others laid a cover of shots to delay pursuit, John and those carrying Joan and Wig ran toward the caverns.

The going was slightly downhill now. The sounds of shooting behind John stopped. The rear guard, having accomplished its purpose, was also fleeing. It caught up. There was a brief halt while the two unconscious forms were transferred to other shoulders. Then they were all running again toward the caverns.

The yawning mouth of the entrance appeared briefly through the trees. A man stood there, signaling. The running group halted while anxious eyes read the arm semaphore message.

"We're cut off," the man next to John spat out. His eyes suddenly jerked to John, widening. At the same instant John felt a sharp stab on the chest. He looked down at the glistening thing of glass and metal, his own eyes wide with disbelief.

He glanced up. The man who had said they were cut off was slowly raising his gun, his face expressionless. And John knew that nothing he could possibly say would make any difference now.

He watched as the small dark opening at the end of the automatic rose and stopped, pointed at a spot above his eyes.

He saw the knuckles wrapped around the gun whiten. The finger hooked into the trigger moved slowly, constricting.

As though in a slow-motion movie, he saw the finger jerk with the trigger. The small black hole disappeared briefly, to be replaced by a white cloud that as quickly vanished. There was a photographic still-life image of a man, the gun lax in his fingers, his eyes fixed on him. Then a roaring, crushing Cosmos sent him reeling at light speed into black oblivion.

CHAPTER NINE

RAG HAD been in her room all morning working on a wedding gown. She hadn't told anyone that she was making it. The materials had been given to her when she was a little girl. She had kept them hidden away until now.

Even in her inner thoughts she was not brazen enough to admit to herself that she was going to make John marry her. She merely recognized inescapable facts. Fact number one, she loved John and no one else. Fact number two, everyone had to get married, at some time or other. Fact number three, she wouldn't marry anyone except John.

The wedding gown was nearing completion. It was sheer white material, the pattern adopted from the latest pictures of such things brought in with other loot from the outside. There were merely ten more ruffles to make and sew on. Then it would be cleaned and carefully put away until the day John proposed to her.

She smiled to herself as she laid it aside. Her thoughts went out, searching for John. In a moment, as soon as she located him, she would get up and leave her room and join him.

Her probing thoughts encountered excited, anxious fragments. She settled on one of them and followed it until she knew what had been happening while she had been sewing.

Alarmed, she probed frantically for John's mind. Her alarm grew as she probed the cavern without contacting him. Still searching, she got to her feet and hurried out of her room toward the radio workshop where she had sensed a great deal of activity.

Just as she reached the door of the radio room a vision rose before her eyes: a man pointing a gun. The gun exploded into action. A roar, and the vision vanished. She knew that what she had seen had been the vivid image in John's mind at that moment. She also sensed that he knew he had been injected with Sepro Nine, and that was why he was being shot.

The vision vanished, but the feel of John's presence remained. He was not dead! Closing her eyes she concentrated all her powers in trying to learn what had happened. He was unconscious. She hung onto her contact, reluctant to let go.

Suddenly she went cold inside. The thought tentacles of *She* were reaching into John's mind as the Sepro took effect. Rag knew the feel of those tentacles only too well, and they sent chills of terror through her.

HER FIRST thought was to break the contact. An instinct forced her to hang on. Never before had she been able to do more than lightly touch the thought probes of *She* without being overcome by dread and revulsion. But now love proved greater than fear.

Whatever happened she must stay in contact with John. The terror made her weak. She sank to the floor, her eyes still closed. Then suddenly her fear left her.

As her fear left her she sensed something in John awaken. John—unconscious. Yet she sensed him lying quietly, analyzing his feelings. She knew when he became aware of her, and felt a warm wave of gladness when he answered her thoughts with his own.

Then he became aware of the thought presence of *She*. Rag felt his first fear, the quick recovery. Without being aware of it she was now, in her thoughts, standing near him. He was on a large bare expanse of granite. Above them was a dark cloud; behind the cloud was a brilliance that pierced the cloud. That brilliance, Rag sensed, was *She*.

John turned his eyes from the cloud and smiled at Rag. She smiled in return and felt something go across from her to him. He seemed to grow larger. Still smiling, he held out his hand. She took it and let him draw her up beside him.

He put his arm around her and drew her closer. Then he looked up at the brilliance of *She* behind the cloud. Rag felt John's defiance and challenge. She felt the radiance beating with ever-increasing fury through the dark cloud.

Then John said, "Tell Kin to tear off the shielding." As in a dream Rag became abruptly aware that she was lying on the floor and someone was bending over her. She heard herself repeat John's words clearly and insistently. Then she was no longer aware of being any place other than with John.

She followed his gaze into the dark cloud and felt the titanic thought power behind it. Impersonal, immense, without form or shape, it reached into her mind and knew her every thought.

Her fear was forgotten. In its place was a growing feeling of awe and worship. Impulsively she tried to drop to her knees. John's arm about her waist held her up.

She felt *She* soften and withdraw slightly, then turn its attention on John. His mind opened. Rag sensed *She* reading in it the conditions John meant to impose, and the weapon he had with which to impose those conditions of conduct.

Abruptly the dark cloud with the brilliance of the mighty thought power of *She* hidden behind it, and John standing beside her, vanished. Rag became aware of voices about her and the humming of motors.

She opened her eyes. She was in the radio room and all the shielding that had prevented any escape of radio waves had been taken off the walls.

"That's it!" a voice shouted gleefully beside her. She looked up and saw Kin standing there, a triumphant grin on his face.

JOHN GROANED at the pain of returning consciousness. A dull throb beat at his scalp. He became aware that he was lying face down on the ground. Groggily he moved his arms forward until he could use them to lift himself up. Every movement was agony.

He rose to his hands and knees and turned until he was able to sit. Not until then did he open his eyes. He stared blankly around him, noting with uncomprehending dullness the dead bodies scattered around.

He put his hand up and felt his scalp. When he withdrew it he frowned at the blood that stained it. Laboriously he climbed to his feet and stood there swaying unsteadily.

He shook his head to clear it and the wave of throbbing pain blinded him momentarily. When it subsided he stood quietly, letting his thoughts gather themselves as best they could.

He remembered being shot and smiled wryly at the realization that the bullet had just grazed his skull. He wondered vaguely how long he had been unconscious.

A movement off to the right through the trees attracted his attention. He studied it, trying to clear his vision so that whatever was moving wouldn't blur. Whatever it was, it seemed to be growing larger.

It loomed in front of him. He blinked his eyes. His sight cleared. There was a man standing in front of him, staring at him curiously. The man wore bright-blue knee-length trousers and a nicely tailored tan shirt.

"You're one of the renegade Individuals, aren't you?" the man asked, his voice apologetic. At John's grunt he continued: "Something very strange has happened. I don't know how to explain it except to say that I seem to have become an Individual too. At least I suppose that must be it, because the way I'm experiencing thoughts—it's almost like when I was a child."

"Ohhh." John expelled his breath in a sigh of relief. Somehow, in some way, the right frequency had been isolated and the whole area was being blanketed with it, destroying telepath contact.

"I—I don't know what to do," the man in front of him went on apologetically. "I saw you and thought perhaps you could tell me what to do."

"Of course," John said soothingly. "Hold me up so I won't fall. I'll tell you which way to go."

JOHN'S HEAD throbbed with almost unendurable intensity now; but he forced his mind to clear. The man assisting him along the path toward the limestone caverns was a new and unguessable factor. John studied him covertly.

His body was well proportioned. There was grace and capableness in the way he handled it. His face was one upon which character could have molded itself very easily, but it was smooth and serene. The eyes, deep blue and clear, were built to twinkle with laughter or fix in concentration; yet they uncuriously concerned themselves only with the task of walking.

The man didn't care where he went or what happened to him! He had no curiosity, no will. All he wanted was someone or something to tell him what to do. Then he was content. John looked at the slight upward curve at the corners of the mouth, an expression of perfect contentment.

A picture rose unbidden in his mind. It was a large city with tall buildings. Its streets were full of people like this man, milling about, asking each other what to do, searching for someone to tell them what to do. Would that be the result if a city were blanketed with waves that disrupted the telepathic bridge across minds?

He remembered Joan's tone of idle conversation when she

asked him if he were going to kill her. Uncurious, polite. And this man plodding beside him had said, "I saw you and thought perhaps you could tell me what to do."

A sickening realization came that even with a weapon that could encompass the Earth and wipe out *She* completely, it couldn't be used if it made everyone as helpless as this man. It would only cause deaths by the millions as confused people made wrong decisions or delayed too long in making any decision in the hope of finding someone to tell them what to do.

John studied the relaxed, docile face of the man. It contradicted everything he had built up about what would happen. And he wondered if it would be possible to develop independence and self-confidence in him.

A shout snapped John out of his discouraged thoughts. He saw Rag running toward him, waving her hand. Behind her came others. In another moment she was in his arms, crying and smiling, her eyes two crystal-blue jewels.

And then John Cole's universe began to spin about him. The world of 1949 mixed itself up with an unreal world of 2436. Kindly people with a twinkle of merriment in their eyes shot each other. Godlike people on whose faces rested the wisdom of the ages plodded dumbly like brutes, obedient to the slightest wish of anyone who cared to direct them.

Cities with mile-high ethereal spires appeared, fragile ornaments adorning the planet. Swift planes darted around the world in less than a day. Floating metal globes, filled with passengers, traveled through the sky or under the sea. Women were used en masse for certain tasks, men for others. And then it changed back to 1949 with its almost squat skyscrapers, snail's pace airliners, and the rush of distracted citizens.

Back and forth, the future and the past, the real and the unreal; and, however mad it became, a pale girl, pathetically small, but with a courage greater than the weight of a mountain, held his huge hand in her own small fingers, guiding...

The mad spiral drew it on itself, speeding its gyrations as it grew smaller. Faster and faster until the past, present and future blurred into one, blended in the sameness without form. Faster, and closer, until there was nothing but a single point. And toward that point John felt himself hurtling through Time and Space.

CHAPTER TEN

"THAT DID it. His temperature's starting to climb now." The words and the voice filtered into John Cole's waking awareness, and slipped away as he tried to grasp their meaning.

"Careful!" A different voice spoke sharply. "Don't be too anxious. After all, if this man was willing to wait for God knows how long for this moment, it would be criminal for us to ruin everything by causing him to die."

"Don't worry," the first voice replied. "Everything's under control. I wouldn't be surprised but what he can hear us right now. Ah! His eyes are moving under the lids."

John opened his eyes. He was lying in the rocking cradle of his sleep chamber. Two men were leaning over him, expressions of anxious concern on their faces. One of them stirred deep memories in his mind.

A miner's lamp cast a mild light over everything. John reached his hand without turning his head to guide it. His fingers encountered the toggle switch, flicked it, and the sleep chamber lit up from the ceiling lights.

Memory clicked, bringing nameless alarm. The familiar man was Old Man Harper who owned the limestone caverns! But it couldn't be.

John turned his head slowly until he could see the instrument panel. His eyes settled on the date meter. The number 1950 beamed at him with glistening whiteness.

John closed his eyes quickly.

"Take your time, fella," the stranger said in a soothing voice.

John explored slowly with his hands. Everything was real. He explored the top of his head. The skin of the scalp was smooth and unbroken.

If it had been creased by a bullet lately, the job of healing had left no scar. And it *had* been creased by a bullet. It wasn't 1950, but 2436. Old Man Harper had been dead for centuries.

John opened his eyes again and explored the sleep chamber. A hole had been knocked in one wall. That was the way he had been found—if this were real and 2436 were just a dream.

It could be real. John knew that Old Man Harper spent most of his time exploring for more caves. He might have found this one, tapped on its walls and found a hollow sound. If he had he would certainly have knocked a hole through to see if there was another cave.

But it wasn't real. It couldn't be. But if not, then what was it? John opened his eyes again.

"I think I'll be all right now," he said.

"Fine," the stranger said. "But don't get up. Some men will be here shortly with a stretcher. We're going to take you to a hospital where you can have expert care. Mind answering a few questions while we wait?"

"It depends on what the questions are," John said cautiously. He reached a hand up to a cross bar above him and gripped it. It was solid metal. He put tension on his muscles. He could see them tense under the skin. He felt his arm pull him up a little.

HIS EYES turned back to the instrument panel. On the lower left-hand corner was a screw with its slot damaged. He remembered now that the screwdriver had slipped on that one and made the nick.

Everything was solid, consistent, and real. But it simply could not be real. Reality was someplace else. In some way, and for some unknown reason, *She* controlled his thoughts now. Of that John was certain.

"How long have you been sleeping?" the stranger asked.

John made a definite decision. If he were wrong, if this were reality and the year 2436 still lay in the future, then he would be considered insane. Yet...

"We might as well get something straight here and now," John said coolly. "This is not the year 1950. It's 2436. I'm not in this sleep chamber. In some unknown way *She* is producing all this illusion to trick me. Well, it won't work. No matter how real it seems I won't be fooled."

"What are you talking about?" the stranger seemed startled. "Of course it's 1950! And of course you're right here!"

John groaned inwardly, searching desperately for some fact or clue to break up this delusion. And suddenly he thought, "Since this is delusion I don't need to be careful. I won't die."

He lifted himself up, his muscles feeling stiff and weak.

"Better take it easy," the stranger said.

John glared at him, then lashed at him with a fist. Surprisingly, it landed on the man's nose. John drew his hand back, feeling the numbness of his bruised knuckles, watching the trickle of blood from the man's nostrils.

"Hey, fella," Old Man Harper growled. "You shouldn't do that."

The stranger put his hand up to his nose. His eyes had a thoughtful light in them. "It's all right, Harper," he said. "I'm beginning to understand something." Then to John, "You're John Cole, the research chemist who disappeared last year, aren't you?"

"I'm John Cole."

"I'm Dr. Forest Lamprey," the stranger said, smiling. He had a piece of cleansing tissue out, dabbing at his nose. "I'm from Chicago, out here for a short vacation. Myself, and my daughter Joan. When Mr. Harper discovered you he went for me right away. That's why I'm here."

"Consistent," John said, "I don't doubt but that I could investigate every word of that statement and find nothing to disprove it."

"You are convinced that none of this is real, aren't you?" Dr. Forest Lamprey asked. "I've noticed you testing things, touching them, doubting even then. You must have a very strong reason for doubting. I've read some of your works and don't think you'd go off the beam. Mind telling me why you think all this is unreal?"

John listened to him with his thoughts growing more and more confused. What was reality? By every test this was reality, but by every test of memory it couldn't possibly be.

HOURS LATER John still didn't know which was reality. Dr. Lamprey had skillfully administered drugs, stimulants, and whatever else was needed, so that aside from continued weakness John was doing all right physically. He had been carried on a stretcher to an ambulance, and then to a hospital in town where he had been often in his capacity of research consultant biochemist. Many of the nurses were those who had been there before.

The local newspaper was brought to him. It was dated August 7, 1950. It seemed authentic. Millions upon millions of minute details held together with the perfect vividness of reality. And still John refused to accept it.

Dr. Lamprey studied him and waited. John was aware of his concern.

"Want to tell me about it?" Dr. Lamprey asked once. When John Cole shook his head Dr. Lamprey shrugged his shoulders and didn't ask again.

"You're convinced I've lost my sanity," John said sometime later.

"Not at all," Dr. Lamprey replied, "The reason I don't

think so is that you are too interested in discovering a flaw in—" he moved his head in a gesture of all-inclusiveness "—all this."

"Then you don't think I'll find a flaw?" John asked.

"I don't think so," Dr. Lamprey laughed. "If such a flaw existed here it would be pounced on at once."

"I could take your statement as a flaw," John grinned. "But I'm sure you didn't mean it the way it sounded. Actually, neither you nor anyone else in this world you think of as reality are in a position to judge. I, perhaps, am. I have two other means of checking. My memories of, say, 1947 or 1948, and my recent memories of 2436. And also, I know the how and the wherefore of the apparent existence of all this that you call reality, including you."

"Care to explain it?" Dr. Lamprey asked quietly.

"You're just as convinced that you exist and this is really 1950, as I am that it isn't?" John asked, knowing what the answer would be.

"Naturally," Dr. Lamprey agreed humorously. "I've been convinced of it ever since I was born—or at least as far back as I can remember."

"Suppose I could prove to you that you don't exist?" John asked. "Suppose I could prove beyond doubt that you were part of a subtle plot to either drive me insane or convince me this is reality, so that I won't try to break free from it?"

"That would take a bit of proving," Dr. Lamprey said. "But I think, coming from a mind as capable of yours, that your arguments would be well worth listening to. I'm interested. And maybe, if you decide to take me into your complete confidence, I can help you prove it one way or another."

"There's one thing against doing that," John said slowly. "If all this is what I think it is, then it is aimed at getting me to do just that, tell you everything, try to prove what I know is true."

"On the other hand," Dr. Lamprey said slowly, "you realize, of course, that your refusal to accept what all of us know is reality can lead you to a mental institution. Could it be that that is the intention of this 'plotter'—for in order for there to be a plot there must be a plotter?"

"I grant that possibility," John replied. "At the same time—oh, what's the use!"

"I think I know how to help," Dr. Lamprey said, his face lighting up with a sudden inspiration. "You just said that a possible motive of this 'plotter' might be to get you to give away some secret. That implies that if you have a secret, whatever or whoever this plotter is, can't get it any other way. Right?"

John nodded without speaking.

"All right then," Dr. Lamprey went on. "Do you know of any secret of chemistry that you feel sure I couldn't know? What I mean is, could you give me an experiment to do with chemicals? Or perhaps you might do it yourself, and if the results differed from those you know are correct, then you will have proved beyond dispute, at least to yourself, that all this is not real."

"How would that help?" John asked. "It would advance my belief no further, one way or another. It wouldn't change your beliefs either, would it?"

"Hardly," Dr. Lamprey chuckled. "Naturally, I know you're wrong. Maybe your ideas arise from some dream you had that still seems very real. You've been in suspended animation for a solid year, with your body temperature around sixty degrees. In that year you could have dreamed up a whole universe based on wish-fulfillment, in which you awakened at some future date such as 2436, which you claim is now the real date. You see that, don't you? And you know that dreams can sometimes be so vivid that, even though we know them to be dreams, they still have all the memory attributes of past reality."

"I see all that," John replied. "I think I'll at least give you part of the picture."

"Fine," Dr. Lamprey said eagerly. "I'll listen until you're through. Then I'll ask any questions that I've thought of while you're talking."

IT WAS THREE days before John finished his story. He had found himself weaker than he thought. Dr. Lamprey had made him stop talking more than once in order, as he said, to digest what had been said. When he finished he relaxed and closed his eyes, waiting for Dr. Lamprey's questions.

"What you say is remarkable, whatever basis I might choose to accept it on," the doctor spoke finally. "Did you ever study the history of philosophy? No? Well, you're in for a surprise then. For a long time, and even today a lot of people believe it, it was thought that there is no reality except thought. The external world, the universe, according to this philosophy, is nothing but thoughts in God's mind, and that even the individual is nothing more than that.

"According to that school of thought there is no matter or substance as we conceive it to be. Perhaps not even time or space in the true sense of the words. The entire universe, all so-called reality, including stars thousands of light years distant, are thoughts in the Universal Mind.

"The individual person supposedly originated, then, as a 'spark' of Divine thought force from God, the Creator. After many incarnations, after many lives, the individual once again merges with his Creator, perfect and immortal.

"What you have just finished telling me, broken down into bare outline, amounts to this: In a time and place which you call 1949 and the sleep chamber where we found you, or its exact double, you went to sleep. That time and that place existed in the material sense, and also that material universe exists at this same moment, but in the year 2436.

"In addition to it, however, a universal mind does exist, but not quite of the type pictured in philosophy. Instead, it is based on physical reality, is actually a functioning of physical matter. It is limited, dependent on a seal of material human brains connected into a positive whole by the action of some unknown chemical that produces perfect two-way telepathy.

"It functions exactly according to the Universal Mind theory, and according to what you say I'm just a thought in this *She,* which I strongly suspect is a carryover from alphabet practice and means Superhuman Entity.

"If that actually were so I don't think there's any way you can break through to actual reality. How do you even know you are you? That's the big flaw in your reasoning. If you are real and we are thought-stuff, how do you reconcile the two?"

"I think you miss the point," John said. "Actually, I'm probably a very sick man right this moment, lying on a bed in the middle cavern of old man Harper's limestone caverns, or maybe in the Cathedral Cavern. That's the physical location of this whole drama being put on for my benefit. You, Dr. Lamprey, and all else around here, are playing on my mind by telepathy, but you are actually resident in parts of the minds of millions of people. You were actually people in 1950, and all this scenery is actual memory of this same landscape as it was in 1950, memory stored in *She.*"

"YES," THE doctor said slowly. "I did miss the point. Actually we can be aware of nothing except thoughts. No matter what impinges on our sensory nerves, we can't be aware of it until it becomes thought. And once it is thought its actual location is indeterminable. Only its location associations, which are also thoughts, can make it seem definitely in one place.

"But I can't quite understand your transition. You say that you had been injected with Sepro Nine, but that a radio-wave blanket was on, blocking telepathy so that *She* couldn't take control. That must have failed, then."

"No," John said emphatically. "I'm sure it hasn't. I don't know why I'm so sure, but I am."

"Maybe we could duplicate that radio broadcaster and knock things loose for you," Dr. Lamprey suggested.

"It wouldn't be the same kind of wave," John said. "By every test we could give it, it would seem the same, but it would not be a physical wave at all. It would be no more real than your nose." John looked at the slightly swollen nose he had punched a few days before and smiled.

Dr. Lamprey rubbed his nose tenderly and returned the smile. "My nose is real to me," he said. "But I see what you mean. It leads to something else we can argue about, though. It's agreed that we can't be aware of anything until it is translated into thought. In other words, we can't become directly aware of a table. We can only become aware of the thought form set up by light waves exciting the retina of the eye. But according to what you are convinced is the truth, everything in this room is already thought form and has no physical reality. It is memory in the universal mind of what actually existed here in 1950. If that is so, then you should be able to be aware of it directly without the use of the senses, for it's already thought."

"But I am aware of it without the use of my senses," John objected. "My physical senses are in my physical body, and if they were bringing me sensations those sensations would be of things in 2436, not 1950."

"I don't know how we're going to resolve this," Dr. Lamprey said. "It was hashed over centuries ago and no way found to break through. The concept of all reality being nothing but thoughts in God's mind is logically unassailable. Its main objection is that it lends little to any understandable theory on how things behave. It's too universal an answer. The theory that physical reality is different from thought, and independent of thought for its existence, is far more practical to work with. All this that I have always thought to be reality is too vast to dismiss as being brought into existence in order to fool you into doing something or not doing something that you can't guess. I'd suggest you forget about it and accept things as they seem for the time being, until you get oriented."

"You think I'm crazy, don't you," John said quietly.

Instead of answering, Dr. Lamprey reached into his breast pocket and drew out an envelope, handing it to John. When John took it, looking at Dr. Lamprey curiously, the doctor turned and left the room, closing the door softly behind him.

Not until then did John look closely at the envelope. In the upper left-hand corner was the return address of the university from which he had received his doctor's degree. A twinge of homesickness stabbed at his heart as he read the familiar name.

His hands shook as he drew out the folded sheets of paper. There was a short letter inside. It stated that attached would be the scholastic history of John B. Cole, Ph.D., plus the personal reports on him from several teachers, as requested.

John started to read. As he read his amazement grew. And when he finally laid the reports down his eyes were wide with disbelief.

CHAPTER ELEVEN

SHE HAD deliberately lied! That incontrovertible fact stood out in John's mind to the exclusion of everything else for the moment. *She* had stooped to deliberate falsehood! Common, cheap lying!

The reports stated that he, John Cole, had majored in philosophy and minored in chemistry, taking his doctor's degree in the history of philosophy. It stated further that, though he had been a brilliant student in all his work, he had been highly unstable and had spent eight months in a sanitarium with a nervous breakdown.

He had actually had only elementary logic and the history of philosophy, both beginning courses, and had studied them only enough to get by on them. And he had never been in a sanitarium for a nervous breakdown.

Yet the evidence as it stood was damaging. And John didn't have the least doubt that if he were able to force Dr. Lamprey to produce the actual records and professors, they would only back up the spurious reports.

That wasn't what bothered him. Unconsciously he had come to believe that *She* was actually godlike. He hadn't realized how complete that belief had become. A mind vast enough to hold all the details of a whole world in its consciousness as pure thought, regardless of its underlying nature, could hardly be seen as less than Godlike. But to lie!

Or was he insane? For the first time since he had opened his eyes, the memory of Rag in his arms still fresh in his mind, seeing old man Harper and Dr. Lamprey bending over him and the year 1950 showing on the date meter, John Cole felt the cold finger of doubt of his own sanity.

If he were insane, then these reports must be true, and he had at one time had a nervous breakdown that he couldn't remember. He would forever live in doubt, suspecting his mad, subconscious powers of rationalizing the irrational.

BUT IF he was sane—and he was, he told himself wildly, trying to still the voice of doubt—then the whole purpose of all this stood out clearly. *She* was deliberately driving him insane, so that if and when he once again returned to waking consciousness in his physical body, aware of his physical surroundings, he would be a helpless pawn in the battle to bring *She* to an end.

Then *She* would triumph. The last of the Individuals would go. For all the future the human race would be immersed in a Universal Mind so that past, present, and future coexisted, and everything that could ever appear real would be nothing but a thought.

The two horns of the dilemma were plain. If he believed his present surroundings, he had to admit he was insane. If he refused to believe them, Dr. Lamprey would be forced to conclude he was insane anyway. In either case he was going to wind up in a nice padded cell in a straightjacket.

Then another thought came. Didn't dilemmas also always prove just the opposite? The conclusion had been reached that in either case he would be locked up and considered insane. How might it be possible that in either case he would be set free and considered *sane?* He took his hand out of his mouth and doubled it into a fist, using the fist for a chin-rest.

The door opened a few minutes later and Dr. Lamprey and two interns came in, worried looks on their faces.

"A nurse reported she heard noises in here that alarmed her," Dr. Lamprey said, "Are you all right, John?"

John stared at the doctor without answering.

"Are you okay?" the doctor repeated, glancing at each of the interns. They started to move slowly to either side.

"Dr. Lamprey," John suddenly said. "Let's assume for the

moment that these reports you got are true in reality, and that therefore I am insane. How would you go about curing me?"

The two interns stopped and looked at the doctor with quiet smiles.

"Why," the doctor hesitated at this new turn, "I would have to think it over before deciding definitely. Perhaps call in a professional friend or two. But I think that in your case the procedure would be to place you under hypnosis and try to make you relive those scenes that are at the root of the disorder. In that way it is usually possible to bring out the hidden frustrations that produced the hallucinations and relieve the mental tension."

"Then I think I have the answer," John exclaimed. "Send me back to that last moment I can remember in 2436. Make me go on from there just another step. If I'm really insane, that should be the means of at least starting a cure. If I'm sane I'll escape from all this. In either case I should become sane again. Right? And…" John's smile was almost imperceptible, "…if I simply vanish without a trace, you'll know I was right."

"Yes," Dr. Lamprey said tolerantly. "If you vanish we'll know you were right. Now, let me give you a sedative so you can sleep. You'll have to have a good night's rest before we can do anything."

"Tomorrow morning then?"

The doctor nodded. John closed his eyes and lay back. He didn't even open his eyes when he felt the prick of the needle in his arm. And just before he dozed off it struck him that there was something familiar about Dr. Lamprey that reminded him vaguely of Gorsh. For that matter, now that he thought about it, there was something about Old Man Harper that made him think of Wig.

"HOW'S THE patient?" Joan Lamprey pressed the

throttle of the station wagon with her right foot. The simple act started the motor, slipped the car into low gear, and shifted gears until the car was gliding noiselessly along the street in high gear.

"He's quite a puzzler," Dr. Lamprey grunted, settling himself comfortably for the drive back to the lodge at the cavern entrance where he and his daughter were spending a much-needed vacation.

"He may turn out to be more of a puzzler than you think," Joan said, her eyes on the traffic. "I had a chance to take a good look at him when he was on the stretcher, you know. I don't think he saw me."

"Yes?" Dr. Lamprey prompted his daughter.

"There was something disturbingly familiar about him," Joan said quietly. "I'd swear I've never seen him before, and yet I'd also swear that I know him better than I know myself."

"All right," Dr. Lamprey said, chuckling. "Tell me all about him. I'd like to know."

"That's just the trouble," Joan said, biting her lip. "It's like knowing something and knowing you know it, but you can't recall it for the life of you."

"Oh, Lord," Dr. Lamprey groaned. "My own daughter, too."

"What's the matter, Dad?" Joan asked, amused.

"Oh nothing. Nothing at all." The doctor gave a hollow laugh. "I'll tell you about it after dinner. Right now I'm too tired."

"OK, Dad," Joan said, flashing her father a tender smile. She had always been very close to her father. She had never known her mother.

He had told her about her mother when she was twelve, nine years before. It had been a bad appendix. They had waited to operate until Joan was born. They had felt it would

THE MAN WHO LIVED TWICE

be safe. But the appendix had ruptured. A cesarean section and an appendectomy were performed almost simultaneously, but it was too late. Her mother had died.

Joan stopped at the mailbox before turning into the dirt and gravel road that led to the lodge. Mr. Harper was always complaining about having to run down to get the mail while his paying guests passed the darn thing a dozen times a day.

There was nothing in it.

AT THE lodge Mr. Harper rushed down the steps to meet them, anxious to find out more about "the boy", as he called him. "Yes sir," he said emphatically. "I remember him. John Cole, he is. Used to hang around here all the time when he was a kid. Haven't seen him since he grew up and went away to college. But it's him all right. I'm sure glad I own that land his cave's on. If he was really in suspended animation for a whole year, that'll be the biggest attraction in the country."

Dr. Lamprey didn't comment. He climbed wearily out of the car and went into the lodge.

"Dad's tired," Joan said. "He'll talk about it after dinner."

"Supper'll be ready right away, young lady," Mr. Harper said. He pulled out his pocket watch and looked at it, then started determinedly toward the back of the lodge.

Joan heard him ordering the cook to hurry up with supper as she followed her father upstairs to their rooms. She knocked softly at her father's door and pushed it open. He was standing at the window, his back to her.

"Something's wrong, Dad," she said, putting her arms around him from behind, and resting her chin on his shoulder. "What is it?"

He reached up and patted her head clumsily.

"Nothing really wrong," he said quietly. "Except that John Cole is insane."

"Oh No!" Joan dropped her arms and retreated a step.

Dr. Lamprey turned and gripped Joan's shoulders. "Yes," he said. "There's no question about it. The drug he concocted to produce suspended animation, or perhaps the year's effect of a body temperature around sixty degrees, or maybe both. He's completely irrational. It was something he couldn't foresee. No doubt he used dogs or other animals in his first experiments. Unfortunately, he couldn't detect any insanity in them when they recovered. Or maybe he didn't look for it and missed whatever signs of it there were. I don't want to talk about it just now."

"All right, Dad. Lie down on the bed. I'll call you when dinner's ready."

She took her father's hand and led him to the bed and pushed him down gently. Then she took off his shoes. When he stretched out she bent over and kissed him tenderly on the forehead.

"Joan." She halted at the door at the sound of his voice. "Tell me about this feeling you had about this young man."

She came back slowly, frowning in concentration. "There's nothing to tell, really," she said slowly. "When I saw his face I just had a strange feeling that I knew every thought in his head. It was like—well, like—like that. That's all," She stopped helplessly.

"Like perhaps you had at one time known him for many years, living constantly with him so that you had heard everything he ever said, and had learned his every habit and mental quirk?" Dr. Lamprey asked without opening his eyes.

"No," Joan hesitated. "Not like that exactly. More like I had been able at one time to read his every thought. More like that. A completeness, if you get what I mean."

"I see," her father said heavily.

She hesitated, but when he showed no further sign of wishing to talk she slipped out, closing the door noiselessly.

CHAPTER TWELVE

MR. HARPER ate quickly. His alert eyes flicked over the table, going slightly bleak when some heavy eater took too much food, mellowing philosophically over the law of averages as they caressed some dainty eater. His lean face and square jaw had reminded more than one person of Walter Houston in his roll of the devil in *The Devil and Daniel Webster.*

His eyes paused speculatively on a young man sitting across from Joan Lamprey. He was some kind of a radio technician. His name was John Kinsey. Only somehow everybody called him Kin. Mr. Harper's shrewd mind had detected from the very first time that John Kinsey laid his eyes on Joan Lamprey that he had fallen in love with her. Once he had overheard them talking. He hadn't snooped, of course, but couldn't help overhearing. And he had heard Kinsey call Joan "Raggedy Ann." She had seemed to like that, too.

Right now, though, Joan didn't seem to have any eyes for Kin. Her eyes were on her plate most of the time, except when they looked up at the doctor now and then, worriedly. This whetted Mr. Harper's curiosity almost to the bursting point. He wished everybody would finish eating so Dr. Lamprey would tell them about John Cole.

His eyes turned back to John Kinsey in furtive analysis. Kin was a very likeable young man. A wide boyish grin that turned on and off, a self-effacing personality like a shepherd dog. The girl he would win would be the one that decided she wanted him and went after him. Right now, for example, he showed plainly that he was hurt by Joan's ignoring him. She *was* ignoring him, too. His eyes pleaded across the table so intensely that a blind horse could have seen it. Her eyes studiously avoided meeting Kinsey's, though. And instead of asking her what the matter was, he just stared all the more and suffered in silence.

Mr. Harper snorted in disgust and turned his attention to Dr. Lamprey. He had known the doctor for over twenty years. The doctor and his young wife had come here for their honeymoon when they were first married.

Joan didn't know that, but Mr. Harper knew. The doctor had cautioned him never to tell her. That was the one secret the doctor kept from his daughter, that his vacations here were sort of pilgrimages to the shrine of his happiest moments.

Something was troubling the doctor now. Instead of being excited about the discovery of John Cole in real suspended animation, as he should be, he seemed to be carrying the weight of the world on his shoulders.

A couple of the guests pushed back their plates.

"Mary!" Mr. Harper shouted peremptorily. "Dessert!"

A perspiring face appeared in the doorway to the kitchen and surveyed the scene with skeptical eyes. With a loud and mutinous "Humph!" the face disappeared. The swinging door fanned a couple of times and stopped. Mr. Harper stared at its expressionless surface angrily, drumming his fingers on the tablecloth.

Mary, with a tray of desserts in her hands, watched him through the crack in the door until the finger-drumming stopped and his hands gripped the edge of the table preparatory to pushing back his chair, then pushed open the door with her generous stern and backed into the room.

Free of the door she turned and sniffed in disdainful triumph at the mixture of emotions on Mr. Harper's face and went at the business of distributing desserts with innocent efficiency.

WITH MOST of the guests nibbling at the desserts Mr.

Harper relaxed a little. Finally he dared to remind the doctor of his promise.

"Oh, yes, doctor," he said as though the thought had just occurred to him. "You were going to tell us about John Cole, weren't you? I imagine everyone," he included everybody with a gesture of his head, "would like to know just what you found out when you got him to the hospital."

Dr. Lamprey looked up from his food with tired eyes. They dropped back to his half-finished pudding. He dipped his spoon in it listlessly, then let the spoon drop into the dish.

"There's nothing much to tell," he said dully. "In the hospital we had him feeling quite well, physically, that is. But his mind..." The doctor shook his head sadly.

"What..." Mr. Harper said, half rising in his surprise. "You don't mean he's insane?"

"I'm afraid so," the doctor said heavily. "He is living in a dream world and is convinced that the real world is imaginary. The usual symptoms. Perhaps a little unusual in their grandeur, but traceable to the infant belief in the egocentricity of reality. He insists that I, you, even the earth we walk on, are all illusions—part of an evil scheme of something he calls *She* which, as nearly as I can understand him, is some sort of superhuman entity or mass mind, equivalent to the medieval theory of reality's being the mind of God and all things being thoughts in His Mind. Only instead of this *She* encompassing the universe, it merely encompasses part of humanity and is trying to take in everybody.

"The pattern is fairly complete, too," Dr. Lamprey went on, "He is convinced that he alone can save humanity from this menace, and that *She* is trying to drive him insane to prevent him from doing it. His background has led him to scientific explanations of it, too. There was some sort of serum called Sepro Nine that produced perfect two-way telepathy between minds. This was used on almost all people on Earth, knitting them into one vast network of living minds that in some ways act as individual minds, and in other ways act as one super mind on a plane of thought above the individual, and that this super mind is *She*. He is also convinced that he has a weapon—some sort of radio wave that destroys this two-way telepathy while it is working, and that if he can get to use it he can destroy or at least control this super mind."

"Well, what do you think of that…" Mr. Harper said in an awed tone of voice. "And do you think he's incurable, doctor?"

"I don't know," Dr. Lamprey said. "We're going to try to cure him. As a matter of fact, John Cole seems very eager to have us try. He seems to think we might accomplish something."

"You mean he knows he's crazy?" John Kinsey spoke up quickly.

"Far from it," Dr. Lamprey tried to explain. "He seems to feel that what will happen when we reach the point where we could effect a cure, if he is really crazy, will be that he will simply vanish before our eyes!"

"You know," Mr. Harper said, "I remember a lot about John Cole when he was a kid. Do you think it would be possible for me to get to see him before you try this cure on him?"

"I hadn't thought of that," the doctor said. "I think it might be an excellent idea."

JOAN LAMPREY tossed restlessly in her sleep, soft moonlight through the window beside her bed, painting a study in light and shadow that any photographer would have given anything to be able to shoot. From the changing expressions on her face, she was having a vivid dream—or nightmare.

Her eyes opened suddenly. She lay still for about five minutes, then slipped out of bed and started to dress. The radium-dial clock showed three o'clock.

She finished dressing, all except her shoes. Turning on the dresser lamp, she hastily straightened out her hair a little. After that she left the room carrying her shoes in her hand.

Stealing noiselessly down the hall, she stopped at a door and slowly twisted the knob. It opened silently. Inside the darkened room she closed the door behind her and stole across the room to the bed. Her arm flashed whitely as she leaned over and shook the sleeping form lying there.

"Kin," she whispered. "Wake up."

"Huh?" came the sleepy response. John Kinsey came awake abruptly. "Joan?" he said. "What's up?"

"Get dressed, Kin," Joan said in a whisper. "I'll meet you down at the station wagon in five minutes, and hurry."

Ten minutes later the station wagon nosed silently out of the dirt and gravel road onto the paved highway into town. Not until then did Joan relax and begin an explanation.

"I have a queer feeling about this whole thing, Kin," she said. "I think Dad has, too. Maybe insanity is contagious."

"You mean about John Cole?" John Kinsey asked. "In what way? The way your father explained it, it's a very standard, cut-and-dried case. Even the cure is standard."

"Yes, I know," Joan said, biting her lip. Her eyes stared bleakly at the ribbon of highway lit up by the station-wagon headlights. "But I saw John Cole for a minute when they were carrying him to the ambulance on the stretcher, and I had a very funny feeling about him."

John Kinsey kept silent.

"Although Dad won't admit it," Joan went on, "I'm sure he had a strange feeling about him too. I couldn't sleep when I went to bed, for the longest time. And when I did get to sleep I had some kind of a wild dream. I can't remember what it was, but I've just got to see John Cole. Right now."

"Why?"

"Because *I'm* crazy, I guess," Joan said in a strained tone.

"You mean you're to sneak into the hospital to see him now?" John Kinsey asked incredulously. "You'll never get away with it!"

"Oh, yes, I will," Joan answered confidently.

And she did. Half an hour later they were standing before the door to the room where John Cole was.

Taking a deep breath, she twisted the knob and walked in, Kin following.

JOHN COLE sat up, rubbing his eyes and blinking in the sudden light she had turned on.

"Hello, John Cole," Joan said with tight nervousness.

"Joan!" John Cole exclaimed. His eyes turned to John Kinsey and lit up in further amazement. "Kin!" he exclaimed. His eyes darted from one to the other, then became confused, "Or are you Joan? You look like Joan, all right, but you seem to be Rag. Which are you?"

John Kinsey sank into the nearest chair. "I don't get it," he said. "I've never seen you before in my life!"

"That's all right," John Cole said soothingly. "Don't let it bother you."

"How did you know our names?" Joan asked.

"Why are you here at this hour?" John Cole asked, ignoring her question.

"I don't know," Joan said frankly. "I don't know why I'm here except that I felt I had to see you before they try to cure you." She bit her lip at the slip she had made.

"Don't be embarrassed," John Cole said kindly. "But please, won't you tell me what it was that brought you up here at three-thirty in the morning? It must have been something very urgent—more than just curiosity to see me before the cure. Unless you feel that I really will vanish when they try to cure me, so this is your last opportunity to see me."

Joan found a chair, dragged it near the bed and sat down. She told him of her strange impression when she first saw him. She told him what her father thought—or at least what he said he thought about him. John Cole listened until she was through. A look of intense sympathy and pity grew on his face as she talked.

"You poor kid," he said when he finished. "But don't worry. When your father works on me in the morning and I vanish, it will all straighten out nicely. You'll all be able to escape this dream trap too, and we'll be back in reality again. Wait and see."

"That reminds me," Joan said. "Dad isn't going to do it this morning. Mr. Harper, who knows you, wants to see you first."

"Old Man Harper?" John exclaimed. "Why? He never did like me. I got in his hair too much."

"He owns the land your hibernating hideout is on," John Kinsey said dryly. "It will be worth money to him to be able to sell circulars with your authentic story, straight from your own lips, as told personally to him, when he opens the place to visitors at so much per person."

"That isn't the reason," Joan said. "Maybe he can really help you, Mr. Cole."

They could hear the night nurse passing on her round. In a few minutes she was due to come into Cole's room so they decided to leave right then.

In the hall John Kinsey whispered, "He really is crazy, isn't he? But how did he know us? I can't figure that."

CHAPTER THIRTEEN

JOHN COLE sat in the dark thinking about the strange visit of Joan Lamprey and John Kinsey and what was behind it.

Beyond any doubt this wasn't reality, even though it could not be distinguished from reality. In the ultimate analysis, it might even be as real as reality itself. Joan Lamprey was a composite. The beauty and build of the Joan in suspended animation that they had been bringing from the small cave where his sleep chamber was located, to the limestone caverns where they were going to use her in their experiment to find a wavelength that would dampen out telepathic sensitivity, and the mind and spirit of Rag. John Kinsey was really Kin. Dr. Lamprey was really Gorsh.

And no doubt Old Man Harper would be Wig. In fact, now that the similarities were apparent, Wig himself was very much similar in every way to Harper as he remembered him from childhood days.

The only thing capable of producing all this was *She*. He had been injected with Sepro Nine and was therefore in *contact,* so all this was the result of that *contact*. In some manner the blanket of radio waves that Kin had started up must have failed.

But if it had, this certainly wasn't what he had been led to expect would result. He was still completely an individual. The only thing different was this substitution of a mental world for the real one. Its setting, 1950, the carefully prepared false scholastic history that convinced these dream characters he was insane, and the authentic detailed elaboration of every minute aspect, all pointed to carefully thought-out purpose—and hence to the accomplishment of some purpose.

Was that purpose to find out the secret of the drug that produced suspended animation? If that was it, then *She* must be unable to get it directly by reading his thoughts. But John Cole shook his head doubtfully over this possible purpose. It somehow didn't justify the means being used.

Was it the apparent one: to actually drive him insane? That seemed weak. Events can't drive a person insane. Events might confuse, but insanity comes from internal causes, not external events.

But suppose now that, with the evidence Dr. Lamprey had that pointed toward his being insane, he was committed to some institution for the insane, and was never able to figure a way out of this dream world? What would happen to his physical body in the reality of the year 2436?

Wasn't he trying to return to it? That was his hope when the doctor put him under hypnosis and guided him back to that physical body—to stay there. If he was unable to, then his body would be undirected. It would be confused and unable to decide what to do. If it were that way, it might ask someone what to do just as that man had done with him when the radio waves destroyed the source of his intelligence.

THAT MUST be it. *She* must be weaving a mental web to enmesh him and hold him, so that from the standpoint of the outsider, the person judging him only by the actions of his physical body, he would be either insane or mindless. Unless…

Here was another possibility. With him nicely sewed up in illusion, some other directing personality might easily, through the mechanism of *contact*, be able to take over and fool everyone into thinking it was John Cole!

Maybe that had been done already. Maybe at this very moment the last few Individuals that had withstood *She* were being betrayed by their belief that he was still master of his body.

He had to get back to it some way.

But how? Actually, of course, he was still in his body. He, his mind, was still the functioning of his neutral circuits. "Getting back", therefore, merely meant discovering how to "wake up".

His eyes turned to the window. How high was it above the street? Suppose he jumped out the window. Since the "body" he inhabited now was nothing more than a thought, dashing it to the pavement wouldn't actually kill him.

The psychological laws governing the functioning of *She's* mind could not have him fall a killing distance and live. The result would be that in this dream world he would become a smashed corpse. Would it also be the means of his returning to reality?

The more John Cole thought about it the more convinced he became that that was the quickest and surest way of solving the problem. After all everyone had dreams in which they were falling. Such dreams always woke a person up, because even in sleep a killing fall that completes itself is a psychological impossibility.

He climbed out of bed and went over to the window in his bare feet. Outside, the lights of the city blinked cheerfully at him. There were so many of them and so many buildings that doubts assailed him. How could all this incredibly detailed picture be anything but real?

He stuck his head out and leaned over. The pavement was at least fifty feet below. If he jumped there would be no possible chance of outliving the fall.

Should he jump? If this were reality, and the world of 2436 were just a dream he had experienced while under suspended animation, and *She* was just a product of that dream, then he would actually die. If this were really Earth in 1950, and he jumped, it would be the end.

JOHN COLE'S face was pale, but there was a light of decision in his eyes. He had to take that chance. He had to trust his mind and believe that in jumping he was going to save mankind. If he delayed he might be too late. He placed one leg over the edge.

"Just a minute, Mr. Cole!" The brittle, clear, masculine voice jerked John Cole's head around as if he had been shot. Standing just inside the closed door of the room, in the darkness, was the figure of a man.

As John hesitated the figure advanced toward him. The feeble light seeping in from the window began to show detail. He advanced until he stood within arm's reach.

"Wig!" John exclaimed, wonder and surprise in his voice.

"At the moment," the man said with a dry chuckle, "I happen to be known as Harper." He held up his hand with a look of mock alarm. "Don't try to prove to me that I don't exist, or that I'm really some character called Wig. You have Dr. Lamprey and his daughter going around doubting everything."

"You're not Old Man Harper, I knew him."

"Turn on the light," Harper said.

John pulled his leg out of the window and crossed the room to the light switch. Then he walked slowly up to Harper, examining him with a puzzled frown.

"You're Wig," he said positively. "You look almost like Old Man Harper looked, but not enough like him to be taken for him. I think I know why, too," he added with a bitter smile.

"Why?" Harper asked.

"I know a little more about things now," John explained. "Old Man Harper was a money-grabbing fool. He had no friends or anyone that loved him. His mind never was in tune with the mass mind, so he had no chance of surviving after he died. His psyche was on a little island all its own."

"Would you believe I'm Harper if I tell you all I know of your childhood, and if Dr. Lamprey and his daughter assure you that they have known me for twenty years?"

"No," John said, shaking his head for emphasis, "I would not. I would still say you are Wig."

"If I'm Wig," Harper said, "why am I in this dream world, while none of the others are?"

"You trapped yourself." John said. He stared bleakly into the man's light blue eyes.

"All right. I'm Wig," Wig, or Harper, answered. "I admire your perseverance and clear thinking. But what are you going to do about it, now that you know?"

JOHN COLE took a walk around the room, frowning in thought. "I don't know," he said. "I'm beginning to see a little more than I did at first, but still not enough. I can see now that *She* permitted the Individualists to survive as a sort of experiment—or maybe insurance—with you as their leader so they would always be under close observation and control.

"They were fed enough opposition in the way of attacks and casualties to keep their independent spirit alive and at high pitch. Probably for several generations that had been going on at a more or less stable level, with the numbers kept pretty well constant, births equaling deaths and casualties."

John stopped at the window and looked out across the city, which was now slowly emerging into the light of early dawn. "And then I came along," he said. "The unpredictable factor out of the past. The possibility that had never been considered. You played along with me nicely, never dreaming that I might have it within my power to destroy *She*. Maybe you didn't think that was possible, until you suddenly saw the puppets of *She* break loose from the strings that controlled them, and begin to wander over the landscape out of control.

"So you plunged me into this world of illusion—this thought world. And you planned to ensnare me here beyond my depth where I couldn't escape."

He turned away from the window. Wig was sitting on the edge of the bed picking his teeth calmly with a broom straw, his eyes watching him with a twinkle of humor.

"My arguments don't seem to impress you very much," John said.

"On the contrary," Wig replied. "However, they aren't quite up to your usual standard. There are several defects in them."

"What, for instance?" John asked.

"First and most obvious defect," Wig replied, "if what you say were true, why is it that Rag didn't sense *She* in me?"

"Possibly because you were there when she was born and she grew up accustomed to the feel of you as you always were," John said slowly.

"That hardly holds water," Wig said. "In your own case she said you positively weren't in contact. How did she know? No, Johnco. You're close. Very close. But there are other flaws in your arguments. Take, for example, the radio frequency wave that is supposed to kill telepathy. Such waves were in quite universal usage at the time Andrew Thorne created the first multi-brain mind. If a radio wave could prevent it now, it most certainly would have made it impossible in the first place, and Andrew Thorne would never have learned the remarkable potentialities of his discovery."

"If those waves are ultra-short, that doesn't hold," John objected. "But suppose that, instead of picking holes in my reasoning, you tell me the answers. And don't give me the old gag that I'm not capable of understanding. I understand *She* quite well now."

"All right, I will," Wig said, sticking the broom straw back in his pocket and getting up.

He walked away from the bed and turned to face it. Then he pointed at it with his finger. Immediately the bed was gone. In its place was an automobile.

"I gather that was supposed to impress me," John Cole said. "It doesn't. The city outside that window impresses me far more."

Wig, unperturbed, pointed again. The automobile became a piano.

"Sit down and play," Wig ordered.

"I don't know a thing about music," John objected. He glanced doubtfully at the piano, then sat down at it and touched a key with a finger. A note sounded, musical and throbbing with rich overtones.

John felt something reaching into his mind. Suddenly he knew he could play. A knowledge of music welled up in him. His fingers, almost of their own volition, began to weave over the keyboard. He listened and marveled. He understood chord formation and sequence, melody, composition. He created his own music. He played the compositions of old masters.

Then suddenly his fingers faltered in confusion. He stared blankly at the keyboard, knowing no more of music than he had before he sat down. He looked up at Wig, puzzled.

And suddenly he knew beyond any shadow of doubt that it was not Wig standing, there, nor was it old man Harper! With desperate swiftness he dived headlong through the open window.

WITH AN involuntary jerk John Cole opened his eyes. The sensation of falling vanished, and with it the awful sight of death in the form of a concrete pavement rushing up at him.

A sense of relief came over him as he realized that he was

once again himself. But was he?

The doubt rose as his eyes came to rest on a girl seated half asleep in a chair near his bed. It was Joan Lamprey! And as he looked she woke up.

"Hello," she said, smiling. "I see you're with us at last."

John Cole stared at her without answering. She went to the door, opened it, and called to someone outside. "He's regained consciousness."

Seconds later Rag came running in and stood at the bed, her eyes filled with tears.

"Go tell the others, Joan," she said. Joan left the room.

"How long have I been unconscious, Rag?" John asked.

"Since yesterday noon," Rag answered. "Almost a whole day. Do you remember? You fainted on the way back here from getting Joan."

"But Joan?" John asked. "I thought from the way that fellow that helped me walk acted, that when *contact* was destroyed they were completely lost."

"They get over it quickly," Rag said. "It's just a temporary confusion. All those within the wave area have gotten over their confusion now and are just as anxious as we are to blanket the whole Earth with radio waves and end the domination of *She*."

"Thank God," John said. "I thought we couldn't do it. I thought from the blankness of that fellow that he didn't have a mind of his own."

He reached up and felt of the turban-like bandage that covered his head.

"I suppose I've been out of my head," he said ruefully. "What a dream I had!"

"It wasn't a dream, exactly," Rag said. "I followed a lot of it. You had a fever. In some way the fever made it possible for *contact* to touch you in spite of the wave blanket. I think fevers make people more sensitive."

"Then I wouldn't have had to dive out the window to get back here," John mused. He told Rag what he had done.

"I don't think you could have helped doing it," Joan said thoughtfully. "Besides *She*, the superhuman entity that exists in the mass consciousness, there is a vast ocean of mind-stuff with no will, subject only to the laws of the mind-stuff itself. You were for the most part lost in it, and that world of 1950 you were in was created from the impulses in your own mind. It isn't delusion. It's very real. I can't explain it, but right now in that dream world you created your body lies crushed on the street. Dr. Lamprey, the Joan and the Kin of that world, and Mr. Harper will go on living their lives, believing that you were insane and killed yourself."

IN THE DAYS that followed, he helped work out the many problems facing them in their battle against *She*. His suggestion on any problem usually turned out to be the one adopted.

A day came when the cavern community was preparing to move en masse to the nearest city, which had now been freed from the domination of *She*.

Johnco had taken a last walk with Rag. They found their footsteps leading them along the path to the small cave, where he had lain in suspended animation for five centuries.

As they drew near, they saw men working on a stone structure that was beginning to take the shape of a large building.

They were met by Wig. "What do you think of it?" Wig asked proudly. "It's going to be the research center to carry on your work in suspended animation, Johnco. This site was chosen so that the place you slept in could be preserved as a sort of shrine."

"Shrine?" Johnco echoed. "Why?"

"Why, he asks," Wig winked at Rag. "If it weren't for

him, the human race would never have been able to free itself from the monster it had unwittingly created by the discovery of Sepro Nine. Thanks to him, the race will once again be free, and the mental forces made possible by controlled use of telepathic union can be used safely. On top of that, he brings us the secret of suspended animation, and all its medical potentialities for good, that will be explored by scientists here in this building. And he asks why we want to preserve his sleep chamber."

Wig looked at Johnco with a twinkle in his eyes. "Do you ever regret having left your own times and traveled across the centuries?" he asked.

"Sometimes I get a little bewildered by everything going on, the complexity of things beyond my grasp with which the rest of you seem entirely at home. Even yet I haven't any idea of the nature of that vast entity called *She*. When Rag talks of creating a counter-entity to control *She* rather than carrying the present program out to its completion, I don't even try to understand." He glanced down at Rag, standing at his side. "But regret being here? I don't think I'll ever regret it. I have that rare thing that was an utter impossibility in 1949. A woman who understands me."

THE END

If you've enjoyed this book, you will not want to miss these terrific titles…

ARMCHAIR SCI-FI & HORROR DOUBLE NOVELS, $12.95 each

D-51   **A GOD NAMED SMITH** by Henry Slesar
WORLDS OF THE IMPERIUM by Keith Laumer

D-52   **CRAIG'S BOOK** by Don Wilcox
EDGE OF THE KNIFE by H. Beam Piper

D-53   **THE SHINING CITY** by Rena M. Vale
THE RED PLANET by Russ Winterbotham

D-54   **THE MAN WHO LIVED TWICE** by Rog Phillips
VALLEY OF THE CROEN by Lee Tarbell

D-55   **OPERATION DISASTER** by Milton Lesser
LAND OF THE DAMNED by Berkeley Livingston

D-56   **CAPTIVE OF THE CENTAURIANESS** by Poul Anderson
A PRINCESS OF MARS by Edgar Rice Burroughs

D-57   **THE NON-STATISTICAL MAN** by Raymond F. Jones
MISSION FROM MARS by Rick Conroy

D-58   **INTRUDERS FROM THE STARS** by Ross Rocklynne
FLIGHT OF THE STARLING by Chester S. Geier

D-59   **COSMIC SABOTEUR** by Frank M. Robinson
LOOK TO THE STARS by Willard Hawkins

D-60   **THE MOON IS HELL!** by John W. Campbell, Jr.
THE GREEN WORLD by Hal Clement

ARMCHAIR SCIENCE FICTION CLASSICS, $12.95 each

C-16   **THE SHAVER MYSTERY, Book Three**
by Richard S. Shaver

C-17   **THE GIRLS FROM PLANET 5**
by Richard Wilson

C-18   **THE FOURTH "R"**
by George O. Smith

ARMCHAIR SCIENCE FICTION & HORROR GEMS SERIES, $12.95 each

G-5   **SCIENCE FICTION GEMS, Vol. Three**
C. M. Kornbluth and others

G-6   **HORROR GEMS, Vol. Three**
August Derleth and others

WHAT LIES IN THE HIDDEN VALLEY?

Are you the superstitious type? Would you be too scared to go into immense, dark, damp forests or great mountains where no man has gone before? Do you tremble at the thought of stepping into places where no one else dares enter?

Come along with a group of daring fortune hunters as they make a leap of faith and embark on a long journey across perilous Korean bandit country…through river rapids, and untouched forests. All the while risking their lives as they head toward uncharted mountains and a valley where flying disks have landed. But was it a valley ripe with treasures of gold…or a valley filled with alien terror?

CAST OF CHARACTERS

CARL KEELE
It's not often you go on a perilous trek into the wilds and end up having to deal with two alien dames who have the hots for you.

HANK POLTER
Leading expeditions through dangerous country and back was child's play to him. But would he make it back safely this time?

NOKOMEE
The only one of the treasure seekers she cared about was Carl—and whether he lived or died would depend upon her.

RANS NOLTI
Armed and ready, he knew the hunt would be full of danger. But would his prowess with a gun save his greedy hide?

JAKE BARTOW
In spite of his assurances to the contrary, he didn't really know where the hell he was taking them. But the statue did…

CARNA
Equivalent of a vamp on Earth, she also had many supernatural powers. She planned to use them all…But for what?

CYANE
This alien scientist held the secret that could save Earth and other worlds from the tortuous rule of the Croen invaders.

VALLEY OF
THE CROEN

By
LEE TARBELL

ARMCHAIR FICTION
PO Box 4369, Medford, Oregon 97501-0168

For more information about Armchair Books and products, visit our website at…

www.armchairfiction.com

Or email us at…

armchairfiction@yahoo.com

VALLEY OF THE CROEN

They say cross-eyed men are bad luck. He stood there, in my doorway, eyeing me up and down with those in-focused black eyes.

His face was hideous even if the eyes had been normal. He was slashed with a wide cicatrice of livid scar tissue from one cheekbone across his nose and down to the button of his jaw on the other side.

He was big, and he looked like bad news to me. I inadvertently moved the door as if to close it, then he spoke:

"You Keele, the mining man?"

I nodded, wondering at the mild voice from the huge battered figure.

"Been looking for you. I've run across something I wouldn't tell just anyone. But I've heard of you, that you are on the level. Here in Korea, you're known already."

I still didn't step back and swing the door wide. But he had aroused my curiosity as well as my natural desire to acquire things. I had made two fortunes and lost both in mining ventures. My present not small income came from an emerald mine in the Andes. It had been a very dirty and very sick Indio who had led me to that emerald mine. You never know!

"I'm pretty busy, could you give me some idea..." I hedged. It doesn't do to seem too anxious or eager in any business deal. Too, the sight of his burly figure, even without the nightmare face, was not exactly reassuring. That bulge under the native quilted coat, I knew was nothing but a gun too big for even his bulges to conceal completely. But a man needed a gun, here. Especially if he had something valuable, such as the whereabouts of gold.

He grinned, and the white, even teeth, and the wrinkles around his eyes took away the sense of impending catastrophe brought by those crossed eyes. I stepped back then, and he walked in. I sat down at my desk. He sat down across from me, and fumbled in one pocket. He lay on the desk an object in wrappings of dirty rags. These he peeled off slowly, his eyes seeming to dart here and there, never looking where they should. As he peeled, he talked:

"I just landed off a ship from Fusan, up-coast. Y' ever been in Fusan?"

I shook my head, watching his fingers work at the knots of the strings around his mysterious object.

"Korea is a funny place. As long as people have been living here, you'd think it would be settled. But it isn't! There're immense forests, great mountains, where no man has gone, places no one enters. They're so dumb they don't even have compasses; they get lost! Think my compass is magic, wonder how I know where to go next, and not get lost. Superstitious, scared to go into the great, dark, damp forests. Scared of the mountains no one has ever climbed. That kind of country is a prospector's meat!"

I nodded. He had the wrappings off, and I leaned forward, a little breathless at the beauty of the thing in his hand. A curiously wrought little statuette about eight inches high, of gold. It was set with real emeralds, for eyes. About the neck and waist of the exquisite female figure were inset jewels, simulating girdle and necklace. A little golden woman goddess! It was very finely wrought, and what surprised me, it was not oriental, not any style of art I could place. Yet it was alien and ancient. I reached for it. He let me take it in my hands, and as I touched it, an electric tingle of surprise, a thrill of utter delight, ran up my arm, as if the image contained a strong little soul intent upon enslaving me with admiration.

"Potent little female, isn't she?"

His crossed eyes were on mine with that queer stare of the cross-eyed. I could make nothing of the facial expressions of this man. He would have been disturbing to play poker against. I would have said he was afraid of that little figure! Afraid, yet very much attached to it. I set it down and he wrapped it up again.

"Strange thing! Tell me about it."

"You know we split Korea with Russia, after the war. I thought I'd take a look around. I have done quite a bit of that. It wasn't hard. Up near the Russian line I found something."

He stopped, looked at me. Whether he was trying to gauge my credulity or my depth, I don't know.

"You're young. You're not yet thirty, Keele; you've got time left to enjoy a fortune such as I'm letting you in on. And I saw such women among these unknown people as no man would believe. I spent a lot of time spying on them."

I figured he was lying about the women to get me to help him finance the trip. But just the same, the hint of unknown and unspoiled beauty of some hidden, weirdly alien tribe of people aroused my curiosity—the old lure of the Savage Princess from kid days, I guess. I hadn't had a real vacation in years—and what would I enjoy more than a jaunt through untouched forests? Toward what didn't matter as long as the hunting was good. And it sounded good!

"Unknown people, virgin forest, beautiful women and plenty of gold. Sounds too good to be true!"

He squinted at me, bared his fine teeth. He leaned forward, almost whispered trying to impress me:

"The people who made that statue are still there. It isn't ancient—they still make them!"

Now I knew he was lying, but still I was hooked. I had to know! For that statue was an infinite evidence of a refinement of art culture rare on earth! If such a race still remained untouched by white man's modern rot—I could pick up a fortune in art objects. I wasn't too dumb to know what they'd bring in New York. I nodded, and he went on.

"I found a cache of valuable gold, jewels, and other things. Things I can't understand. I could be better educated, Mr. Keele. That's why I've come to you. I want some help."

I leaned back. If he found gold, he should have the wherewithal to get in there and back without my help. So he was lying. I determined to find out why, and just what the lie was.

"Go ahead," was all I said. Give a liar enough rope and he'll trip himself.

But he didn't! He didn't ask for money! He only wanted me for advice, for the names of experienced men of the kind he needed, to help him go back there. Men willing to fight if needed. Or else he was too clever. At the end he had me. I was committed to supervising and accompanying that expedition. Or was it the wise emerald eyes of the little golden Goddess that trapped me? I didn't know, then.

Finally I got it out of him. He hadn't brought back the gold. He had to cross bandit territory, and he didn't have to tell me why he didn't carry his fortune with only his own rifle to guard it.

I picked two well-known men who were available just then. Hank Polter had led more than one hunting party through country I wouldn't have picked—and come out safe. He knew what a gun was for, and when to use it. And that's the most important part of handling a gun, knowing *when* you have to shoot, and then doing it first. The man that shoots before he has to is going to get you into more trouble than he can get you out of.

Lean and tough, he knew the ropes. Around thirty, just under six feet, not bad looking, he was making the most of

Seoul's wide-open hot spots. Nearly broke, he jumped at our offer.

Seoul is the capital of Korea, in case you don't know. Everyone did pretty much as they pleased, for there were few restrictions from the so-recently installed government. There are a number of gold mines around Seoul, which was why I was there. Like the cross-eyed Jake Barto, I knew that something would turn up worth owning where governments have changed three times in as many years.

Frans Nolti, the other hunter we hired, was more of a fortune hunter, by appearance, than one who knew his way in the jungles of the world. Handsome in his Italian way, he was suave, apparently well educated, very quick in his movements. He gave the impression of extreme cleverness, of intellect held in reserve behind a facade of worldliness, of light clever talk.

Both of them knew their Orient, far better than I. Which was one reason I wanted them.

Barto had at first wanted a large party, at least a score of "white" men of the western school, able to fight and smart enough to know how. But I had talked him out of it.

"You see, Jake, with two like these, we can travel fast. If there's treachery, if they aren't satisfied with the cut we're offering, why it's two against two—you and I have an even chance. With a larger party, we might pick up some scoundrels who will try to murder us and make off with the treasure. Providing we *get* the treasure!"

Jake eyed me, in that maddeningly unreadable cross-eyed expression of cold ferocity which the scars gave his ugly face. We had agreed on one-third each, the other two to split the other third between them. I was footing the bills, Jake was nearly broke. He had found the stuff, and tried to hold out for half, me a quarter, the other two to split a quarter. I said nothing doing.

"No, Jake, this first trip, it's got to be this way. If it's like you say it is, there'll be more. What we can carry won't be all the value. There'll be more to be gotten out of that ruin than the stuff you found. You'll have the money to do it, after this, and it's your find. We'll be out, after this one trip."

We sailed up the east coast of Korea from Fusan to the village of Leshin. By native cart from there to the ancient half-ruined city of Musan. That's close to the Manchurian border. There we hired eight diminutive Korean ponies and four men to "go along" as Barto put it, for they didn't want to go, and didn't appear like men of much use for anything but guides. And Barto knew the way. But I didn't want to be wandering around without any native interpreters, without contact of any kind possible with the people we might encounter. None of them had been more than a few miles into the wilderness. They were sad looking men when we started northward. But Koreans manage to look pretty sad much of the time. With their history, that's easy to understand.

Something about the burly, ugly Barto's behavior began to worry me. He didn't know where he was going. He had told a lie, but just what the lie was I couldn't figure out. I watched him covertly. Whenever we came to the end of a march, instead of sighting his landmarks, making sure of his bearings—he would go off by himself. Next day, he would know exactly where he wanted to go—but sometimes the "way" would be across an impassable gorge, a rapids, or straight into a cliff.

One night, the fourth day and well into the wilderness, we were moving up a broad valley through a forest of larch. I sighted a deer, and called a halt while I stalked it. I got it, and came back ahead of the rest, who were cutting up the deer. I moved quietly in the woods—it's a good habit. I came upon

Barto, and he was oblivious of me. He had the little golden girl in his hands, talking to it.

"Now, tell me the way, girl, tell me the way." Then he held the girl loosely in his hand, as I watched, it gave me an eerie feeling to see the little figure turn, its outstretched hand pointing northward like a compass. Was Jake Barto a madman? Or *did* the little figure act as a compass? If so, why did Barto have to rely on the pointing figure's hand for directions? If he didn't get that figure from the place we were heading, where did he get it? How did he know there was anything of value in the place we were headed for?

These questions tormented me, for I could not ask them without revealing to Jake that I knew he was lying. And that meant a showdown. I might have to kill him. Still, I had to get the truth out of him, or let a madman lead us on and on into an untracked wilderness, if that is what he was.

For several days we did not see a sign of life, after that deer.

The forest became denser at every mile, with more and more swamps and surface water. Time after time our ponies mired and had to be lifted out of the mud. Lush ferns and rank grass made walking dangerous. The trees were interlaced with draping festoons of gray "Spanish moss," forming a canopy overhead which let through only a gloomy half-light. No sounds broke the stillness except the half-awed calls of the men. No birds, not even a squirrel. Then it began to rain.

That drizzle continued for a week! The men became frightened at the gloomy stillness and exhausted by the strenuous work of keeping the ponies moving.

Then in the night my four Koreans deserted. They didn't take any ponies, just what grub they could pack. We all felt better off without them, but I often wonder if they ever found their way out of that morass.

The next day there came a break. We sighted a majestic mountain about two days' march ahead. It looked like a gloomy cloud that had settled to earth for a moment's rest. But no cloud ever managed to look so rocky, so windswept, or so welcome. And no patch of blue sky ever looked so good as that sky above the mountain, swept clean of the rain curtain by the updraft.

Jake seemed to recognize that mountain, gave an audible sigh of relief when we sighted it. My suspicions quieted.

We went hunting that day. It was the first dry camp in a long time, the first signs of game; we needed a rest. As usual, Barto stayed at camp to guard the ponies and camp equipment.

We were on the trail of a bear when we saw a strange object in the sky. It looked like a doughnut or a saucer, and it settled to the earth on the far side of the great white mountain at whose foot we had made camp. It seemed only an hour's walk to a point where we could overlook the landing place of the strange object, and Hank and Frans pushed ahead, curious and a little frightened. I had read in the American newspapers the accounts of "disk ships" and knew they would not be able to get close to it, and I wanted to watch Hank. I let them get out of sight, then turned back to camp. Quietly, I was nearing our camp, when the scream of a woman in pain came to me!

It was the answer to all my apprehensions about the ugly Barto, a sudden materialization of the vague distrust I had felt all along! I broke into a run, crashing through the young, white birches and larches, to the clearing.

A chuckle reached me, a gloating heavy laugh of triumph.

Barto had the girl prone, one arm bent near to breaking, her knees caught beneath his weight. I caught him by the shoulders, heaved backward, sent him sprawling across the young grass. He sat up, glared for an instant, then went for his gun. Before it came out of the holster, my foot caught him beside the jaw. He was too big for any other method I might have chosen to be effective. The kick stretched him unconscious; my heel had struck the button.

I turned, to see the girl disappearing among the brush. She had darted away instantly she was free. That she would bring her people down on us I had no doubt. I did doubt their ability to hurt us. Unless she belonged to a band of Manchurian bandits hanging out here in the wilderness, they would not have arms. In the case she was of the bandits, we might be wiped out in our sleep.

I bent over Jake, hoping I had not broken his neck. He looked as though he would be out for some time. I picked up his heavy .45, shoved it in my belt. I wished Hank and Frans would return soon. The four of us might be able to handle her people.

I turned—and *she* stood there, looking at me!

That such as she existed among the usually ugly Koreans and Manchurians was impossible! I gasped a little in unbelief. Her clothing was like nothing on this earth.

Soft green leather was clasped low on her hips with a narrow gold band, set with jewels. It was a skirt, I suppose, but it hung with a diagonal hem-line running from hip to knee, it was beaded in an intricate pattern, not Oriental, somehow reminding me of American Indian bead work.

On her feet leather sandals, laced like the ancient Greek sandal nearly to the knee. In her hand a bow of horn, small and powerful. Around her shoulders a short leather cape similarly beaded and fringed. Around her brows a jeweled circlet set like a diadem, and it crowned a young queen, proud and knowing very well her beauty and its power.

Her features were neither Caucasian nor Oriental, certainly not the heavy-boned native stock. I couldn't pin them down to any race. Her nose was straight, the nostrils neither wide nor narrow, but strong and firm. Her eyes were too wide-set and heavy-lidded to be Aryan, but they were not tilted; they were level. Her hair was not black, but chestnut and curled or naturally very wavy. Her glance was tawny and aflame with anger and excitement, furious upon the prostrate Barto. They were very light-colored eyes, and they caught the sun in a blaze that made them seem yellow.

Striking, she was a figure not of any ordinary kind. Her every aspect told that she came of a culture unknown to me. She was evidently not ignorant, but of a different way of life.

Looking into her eyes, appraising her interest in myself that had brought her back, drinking in the immense appeal of her strangeness and her evident gentility—the evidences of a past of cultivated living as strange as her attire—I forgot the unconscious man at my feet.

Her skin was whiter than my own! Her arms were bruised purple where Barto had clutched her. Then she spoke, in halting Korean:

"Is he dead?"

"No," I answered.

"Then he will live to meet a far worse fate! I know why you are here, stranger, and I warn you! You are on a fool's errand! The Golden Goddess is death for such as you!"

I was bewildered.

"What Golden Goddess?"

"The Golden Goddess whose symbol led him here. He does not know what it is. He stole it by murdering one of our own messengers for it. He did not *know* at all; he only heard the tales that some relate about her. They are false tales."

"Did he tell you how he got it?"

"He was boasting to me, trying to get me to tell what I knew about her dwelling-place. I would not, that is why he hurt me."

"Why did you come back, whatever-your-name?"

"My name is Nokomee, and I came back to tell you something you need to know. Leave these others, and you will live! Stay with them, you will be slain with them. We do not allow such as he to come among us, golden girl or no."

"I cannot leave my comrades because of danger. What kind of man do you think me?"

"I do not care! I can only tell you. This is a secret place, where we remain hidden from the men of earth. I know what happens to those who stray upon our secrets! Go, and think no more to pry into treasure tales of this mountain land. It is not for such as you. Go, before it is too late. I cannot hold back the death from you."

I laughed. I thought of the Koreans who had deserted, of their talk about the fires at night, of demons and haunted mountains ahead.

"We came a long way on the track of Barto's tale of treasure from which he brought the golden girl. It will take more than words to frighten us away."

"Do not laugh! I try to save you from something even worse than death that can come to you. I want to return to you the favor that you did me. If you do not listen to me, how can I help you?" Her voice took on a plaintive, charming note; she smiled a half-smile of complete witchery.

A high, keening cry came suddenly from the slopes above us, and she raised on her toes as if to spring away.

"They come, my friends! I must leave you. I can only tell you to stay close by your fire at night. I cannot say what fate will strike you. I cannot help you. Go back, friend who would live, go back!"

She turned and sprang lightly up the slope toward the sound of the cry, half human, half beast-like, that she had called "her friends." It had sounded to me like the cry of a wolf, or a cat-man, anything but human. But people can make odd sounds, and imitate beasts. Still it had been an eerie sound that gave me a foreboding, added to her warning words. What kind of people were these, who wore leather and jewels and used bows that might have come off an Assyrian wall painting?

Came a tumult above, the high clear blast of some horn, a dozen eerie cries hardly human—a rush and a pounding in the earth as though a party had ridden off on heavy, full-size horses. No Manchurian pony ever made such a sound on soft ground!

Polter and Noldi came back about an hour later. I had dragged the big Barto into a tent and made him comfortable. He was snoring peacefully. Polter squatted down beside me, folding his long form like a jackknife.

"That thing *was* a ship, Keele," he said. There was a husky excitement, repressed but still obvious about him. I grunted.

"It landed among some big timber on the south end of the mountain. We got pretty close, enough to see the sides of the thing. Men busy around it, we couldn't get too close, afraid they'd see us."

I started, a pulse of unreasoning fear, of terrific interest, ran through me. I asked in a voice I couldn't keep calm, "What kind of men, Hank? I saw reports of such ships in the papers, no one got close enough to see *that* much. Newspapers called them illusions!"

"They're not our kind of men; they are something very different. I don't know just how to tell you, besides I couldn't be sure. But they seem to be a people—" He stopped. "I'd rather you'd see it yourself. You wouldn't believe me."

Noldi came out of the tent where Barto was still snoring. He came over and squatted across the fire, eyeing me strangely.

"What happened to the big jerk, Carl?" he asked, a little tremor of anger in his voice.

"I've got to tell you fellows we're in trouble," I began. I did not believe that the girl's people would ignore Jake's attack upon her.

Hank looked at the slender man from New York's East Side. "What's the matter with Barto?"

"S'got a bruise on his jaw the size of a goose-egg. Like a mule kicked him. Scratched up quite a bit. I just wondered. He's unconscious, too; I couldn't wake him up."

"We may be in for it," I went on. "When I got back to camp, Hank had a girl. He'd thrown her down, was struggling with her. I had to put him asleep to stop it. Didn't want trouble with her people."

Noldi glanced at the torn place in the soft sod where the scuffle had taken place. I had unconsciously nodded toward it. He got up, walked over, picked something out of the grass.

"Some girl, wearing this kind of stuff!"

He handed the glittering bauble to Polter. It was a necklace of emeralds, with a pendant of gold in which was set a big blue stone that I couldn't recognize, maybe a diamond, maybe something else. It looked almighty valuable, each stone was as big as a man's thumbnail. It had snapped, lain there unnoticed by either of us.

Noldi looked at me a little venomously.

"Looks as if you were a little premature, letting her go. We should have found out where she gets this kind of sparkle first!"

"Seemed the safest thing to do. We are only four, how could we handle her friends?"

"Bah, they wouldn't have known where she was. We could have kept her till we were good and ready to let her go."

I stood up, took out my pipe and filled it.

"What about this ship you saw, and the people around it. That's important, not this girl and her jewelry."

"We couldn't see much except that it was a ship and that it landed in the trees where it couldn't be seen from the sky. It's pretty big, and there are men moving around it. That's all."

"That's plenty! If we run into them, there is no knowing what they'll do. That ship was never built on this planet."

Noldi didn't smile or laugh. He just looked at me. Serious, puzzled, and a little scared.

"You think it's a space ship, eh, Keele?"

I nodded.

"What else could it be?"

"What's it doin' out here in no man's land?" Polter asked. "You'd think strangers like that would land near a city, try to make some kind of official contact."

"If you were landing on a strange world, would you land near a city?" I asked.

Polter laughed.

"I guess you hit it. They don't know whether they'd be welcome or not. Scared, eh?"

"Just careful, I'd say. We don't know anything about them. But ships like that have been reported off and on for hundreds of years. Don't be surprised if you never see a trace of it again, and if no one else but me ever believes you when you mention it. I don't think we'll have to worry about the flying saucer."

"What the hell do they want, then?" Noldi didn't know what I meant, exactly.

"Nobody knows, Frans. Nobody ever saw them as close as you just did today."

Watching Jake Barto next morning, I saw that the little image in his hand pointed right across the center of that cloud-topping mountain. That meant we had to go around it, for we were not equipped for such climbing, nor would there have been any sense in it. Jake figured on circling to the left, and I was glad, for I for one wanted no parts of that disk ship that Polter and Noldi had seen in the other direction. Jake ignored me. He was unpredictable!

It was a long mountain, and we traveled along one side, toward the north, figuring on crossing to the east wherever a pass appeared. After a time a faint trail showed, and we followed it. It drew us higher, until we were moving perilously along a ledge of rock, with precipitous walls above and a sharp drop below. Higher and higher, above the tree-line now, the path went on, and there were signs of travel along it that worried me.

Polter was in the lead, and as we rounded a shoulder of rock, gave a cry of wonder. We hurried after, to see the trail breaking over a low crest of the mountain, and leading now downward. This shoulder of rock outthrust here marked the place where the trail we were following crossed the ridge of the mountain crest at its lowest point. But it also marked something else, which was what had caused Polter's cry.

A line of dust across the trail and along the near-bare rocks stirred and lifted and fell fitfully, as if the air was barred passage by some invisible wall, and there were the skeletons of birds that had flung themselves against the invisible wall and died, falling there. There was the skeleton of a goat half across the trail; and at one side, what had once been a man! All these dead—and the bones could be seen here and there along the far line of the dust—had gone so far and no farther. Polter had stopped fearfully ten feet from the clearly marked line—and I for one had no desire to add my skeleton to the others.

For a few minutes none of us had anything to say, then reason reasserted itself, and I pressed past Polter, knowing that the thing was an illusion born of coincidence and wind currents. Some baffling current of wind around the mountain formed here a wall of air cleavage, and the skeletons were merely coincidence. I pushed up to the strange line of lifting and falling dust, a little roll showing the magic of invisible force, and pressed on, as if to cross.

Behind me a cry gave me pause. I turned, looking for that cry's source, for it seemed to me the cry was the girl I had rescued from Barto. That saved me, for the little horse behind me pressed on across the strange line—and faltered, gave a horse-scream of terror, fell dead before me.

We stopped, terror of the unknown in our breasts, wondering—afraid to put the wonder into words. We did not look at each other or discuss the thing, we just accepted it, and stared dumbly at it like animals. I tossed a rock across the body of the now quite motionless pack animal, the rock reached the wall beneath which my animal lay dead—slowed, curved sharply to the ground, did not roll, but lay as if imprisoned in invisible jelly!

There was a wall of invisible and deadly force there, and there was no known explanation for it!

I growled at Barto, all the suspicion and distrust that had been building up in me toward him in my voice.

"What does your golden girl tell you now, Jake?"

Jake surprised me. He walked ahead toward that frightening manifestation of the unknown, holding the little statuette before him like a sword, his ugly face rapt in some listening beyond me. As the little statue crossed the line, he sang out:

"Listen, Goddess of the Golden forces, listen and heed! We come from afar to pay our worship, to give to you our devotion, and we are met with this wall of death! Is that the way you greet your friends?"

Jake waved the statuette in a circular motion, then crossed the circle twice with the waving gold. He stood there, his crossed eyes darting here and there along the line of force, and after a long minute, after a time that seemed filled with a distant chuckling, like thunder too far off to be heard clearly—the lift and fall of the dust on the baffled wind stopped, the strict line of the wind's stoppage began to disappear, the line of demarcation was gone!

Jake reached out an arm, feeling cautiously for the invisible wall, and after a minute, his face lightened from its habitual gloom, he stepped across the line, and did not stagger and fall as had the horse. The wall was gone! Jake turned, said calmly:

"Come on, our friends have decided to let us in."

My mind in a whirl at the unexpected display of knowledge beyond me, of forces beyond the power of any rifle bullet to overcome, of strange hidden things here—I stepped across the line, keeping close to the tracks left by Jake's big feet. Polter and Noldi followed and the horses plodded after. We trudged on, but not the same. We were afraid, and we were conscious of a vast ignorance, of a fear that we did not belong here, that the only wise thing for us to do was to turn back and give up this Jake Barto and his cross eyes and his mumbo jumbo statue to his own doom.

At least that's the way I felt, but something stronger than curiosity drew me on. I wanted to know why I was so drawn when reason kept demanding I give up this quest. I wanted to know why a golden statue pointed always to one point on the horizon, and why that wall of force had obeyed Jake's injunction to go away. Or was I unable to think, really? Was I shocked out of my ability to reason and act on my reason's dictates?

Ahead, as the trail dipped low, a vast panorama of valley and hill and hollow, of eerie rocky spires, lay outspread. Here and there were cultivated fields, and figures at work on the fields. In the distance shone a stream. It flowed meandering into a wide lake. There were two villages, not clear in the haze. At the distant lake, some kind of larger structure lifted tall towers, shining with prismatic glitter, a city of strange appearance.

We had crossed a barrier, and we had entered a land of the living—but it was unclear before us. The drifting mountain mists, the sun-glitter and the haze of noon kept the scene from striking through to our brains with its true significance. For there was an eerie *difference* about the scene; it was not a land below us such as any of us had ever seen. I felt that and yet I could not think clearly about it. We moved along like zombies, not thinking—just accepting the unusual and the unknown as casually as if we were travelers who could not be astounded. But inside, my mind was busily turning the significance and the meaning of this wall of force. I had heard of such walls before—upon Shasta in California, and in Tibet, and in ancient times in Ireland, and there were other instances of a similar wall in the past, and in the present in other places. But what it could really mean, that was what I did not know.

After crossing that invisible barrier, things began to happen in a sequence, of a strangeness and with a rapidity such that I was unable to analyze or to rationalize. From there on I was like a man on a tightrope, hounded by invisible tormentors trying to shake me off. I had not time to wonder whether it was true that spirits existed. What I did think was that some of these Korean primitives had a Devil Doctor who surpassed all others in trickiness, and was amusing himself at our expense. But I did not *think* it, I *clung* to the idea to save my reason from tottering over the brink.

The first thing after the wall that could not exist but did— after we had passed on over the ridge and half way down the mountain side—was a gully along the mountain side, up which Barto turned. I assumed he was still following the pointing of the magnetic statuette, but I was vaguely conscious that none of us were *really* conscious—were under a kind of spell in which our actions and our thoughts were predetermined—inevitable! I knew it, but I could not shake it off, nor put my finger on any reason why I should shake it off and call a halt to the strange, wordless, silent following of Jake and his eerie talisman.

The faint trail led along the bottom of the gully, and after twenty minutes of downward progress, led into a dark overhang of rock, the sky hardly visible where the rocks almost met overhead. Down the semi-cavern we went; still silent, zombie-like; and I felt ever more strongly the compulsion that made us so move and so unable to do otherwise.

Jake was striding rapidly now, his dark ugly face aflame with weird eagerness, my own heart pounding with alarm at the strangeness and the irrationality of the whole proceeding. He held the statuette out stiffly, it seemed fairly to leap in his hands, as if tugging with an ecstatic longing to reach the dark place ahead. The rocks closed completely overhead; the dimness changed to stygian darkness. I got out my flashlight, sent the beam ahead. But Jake was pressing on through the darkness, directly in the center of the trail.

Quite suddenly the cavern turned, opened ahead, wider and wider—and before us lay a room of jeweled splendor, the temple of some forgotten—*or was it forgotten?*—cult of worship.

The golden statue in the center of the big round chamber drew our eyes from the splendor of the peculiarly decorated walls, from the strange crystal pillar on the tall dais at the far wall, from the weird assemblages of crystals and metals that had an eerie resemblance to machines—to a science entirely unknown to modern men. All these details of that chamber I remember now, looking back, but then—my attention and that of the others was entirely drawn to the beauty of the tall, golden woman who stood in frozen metallic wonder at the center of the forgotten crypt.

Jake, his ugly face in a transport, had fallen to his knees, was crawling forward to the statue abjectly, mouthing phrases of worship and self-abnegation. Close on his heels came Polter and Noldi, eyes rapt, movements mechanical. I stopped, some last remnant of sense remaining in my head, and by a strong effort of will held my limbs motionless.

As Jake reached the statue, the little golden replica of the life-sized woman of gold seemed to leap out of his reaching hands, and clung against the metallic waist of the golden woman as a lodestone to the mother lode.

Even as Barto's hands touched the statue, he slumped, lay there outstretched, his fingertips touching the metal hem of the golden skirt; and whether he was unconscious from unsupportable ecstasy or for what mad reason, I did not know, but I did not *want* to know.

Undeterred by Jake's condition, the two men following in his steps also reached out hands to touch the golden metal—and fell flat on their faces beside Jake Barto, unconscious, or dead!

I stood, numb and with a terrific compulsion running through my nerves, which I resisted with all my will. I drew my eyes from the strangely pleasant magnetic lure of the metal woman with an effort and examined that strange chamber.

The walls were covered with a crystalline glittering substance, like molten glass sprayed on and allowed to harden. Behind this glasseous protective surface, paintings and carvings spread a fantasy of strange form and color, but the light was too dim to make much of it, except that it was alien to my experience, and exceedingly well done, speaking of a culture second to none.

Beyond the central form of the strange golden statue, was the dais which I had noticed at once, and now my eyes picked out the fact that on it was also a glasseous protective sheath about a form—another statue, I thought.

Thoughtfully I prowled along the rim of the room, examining the wall frescoes foot by foot, seeing on them a strange depiction of semi-human forms, of crab-men and crab-women, of snake-men and snake-women, of men half-goat and half-man, of creatures hardly human with great jaws that looked like rock-cutters, with hands like moles on short powerful arms, fish people with finned legs and arms, their hands engaged in catching great fish and placing them in nets, a nightmare of weird half-human shapes that gradually brought to me a message that I could not accept.

If that rock painting was telling a true story and not some allegorical fantasy—these people who had built this place had been a race who knew the secrets of life so intimately they could manipulate the unborn child into shapes intended to give it powers and physical attributes fitting it for amphibious life, for the underground boring life of a mole, for the tending of flocks in the goat-legged men—the whole gamut of these monstrous diversions from the normal human seemed to me designed—purposely—to build a race which, like ants, has a shape fitted to its trade.

I threw off the illusion of a deformed past race the wall art gave me, and passed on to examine the crystalline pillar on the dais. I stood a long time, before the dais, drinking in the beauty of the form locked within the prisoning glass.

No human, no earth woman—she was different from anything I had ever even imagined.

Female, vaguely human in form she was, with an unearthly beauty; but four-armed, with a forehead that went up and up and ended in a single tall horn, as on the fabled unicorn.

Her eyes were closed, if she had eyes beneath the heavy purple-veined lids, so like the petals of some night-flower, pungent with perfume.

Naked the figure was, except for a belt of what looked iron chain around the waist, black and corroded with time, holding her with a great bolt and link to the side of that crystalline prison.

Her hair, black as night, was pressed tight to the skull by the pressure of the crystal, which must have been poured about her in a molten or liquid state.

As I stood there agaze at the strangeness and wonder of her, a voice at my shoulder made me whirl in surprise. A soft, silky familiar voice:

"Do you find the dead Goddess so fascinating, stranger from the world of men?"

It was the girl of the forest, no longer in hunting garb, but dressed in Turkish trousers, vest and slippers with upturned toes. Jewels glittered about her waist and neck and arms, her wrists jangled with heavy bangles, in her ears two great pendants swayed—her eyelids were darkened and her lips reddened. She was a ravishing houri of the harem, and I gasped a little at the change.

"Have you put on such clothes for my benefit?" I asked, for I really thought perhaps she had.

She frowned and stamped her foot in sudden anger.

"I come here to save you from what has happened to your friends, and you insult me. Don't you want to live? Do you want to become what they are going to become?" She pointed to the bodies of Jake and Noldi and Polter.

I turned where she pointed, to see a thing that very nearly made me scream out in revulsion.

I shuddered, shrank back; for several creatures were bending over the three, lifting them, bearing them away.

It was the strange, revolting difference from men in them that caused my fear. Once they may have been men, their far-off ancestors, perhaps—or in some other more recent way their bodies had been transformed, made over into creatures not human, not beast, not ghoul. What they were was not thinkable or acceptable by me. I turned my face away, shuddering.

They were men such as the wall-paintings pictured, something that had been made from the main stock of mankind, changed unthinkably into a creature who bore his tools of his trade in his own bone and flesh. Mole-men, men with short heavy arms and wide-clawed hands, made for digging through hard earth. They bore my friends away on their hairy-naked shoulders, and I stood too shocked to say a word. Three mole-men, accompanied by three tall, pale-white figures, figures inexpressibly alien—even through the heavy white robes—that moved with an odd hopping step that no human limb could manage, turned their paper-white, long, expressionless faces toward me for an instant, then were gone, on the trail of the mole-man. Beneath those robes must have been a body as attenuated as a skeleton, as different as an insect's from man's. Within those odd egg-shaped heads must have been a mind as alien to mine as an ant's mind.

"Why do your people take my companions?" I managed, when I had regained my composure.

"They are not my people; they are of the enemies of the Dead Goddess." The girl gestured to the figure in the crystal pillar. "My people have no time for them, but neither have we power over them. They go their way, and we go ours. Once, long ago, it was different, but time has made us a people divided."

"What will become of the three men?"

"They will become workmen of one kind or another. Everyone works, in *their* life-way. But it is not *our* way! They guard our land from such intruders; we let them. It is an ancient pact we have with them."

"Why did they not seize me, I am an intruder as much as the others?"

"Because I signed to them to let you stay. You did not see, whatever-your-name-is…"

"Call me Carlin Keele, Carl for short. What is your name, and what is your race, and why are you so different from people as I know them?"

"My name is Nokomee, as I told you before. You are still confused from the magic that led you here. I have saved you once, and *now we are even*; my debt to you is paid. You will never see your friends again, and if you do, you will be sorry that you saw them, for they will have become beasts of burden. Now go, before it is too late. This is not your kind of country."

Something in her eyes, something in the sharp peremptory tone she used, told me the truth.

"You don't really want me to go, Nokomee. I don't want to go. Many things make me want to stay—your beauty is not the least attraction. I could learn so much that my people do not know, that yours seem to know."

"I would not want my beauty to lead you to your death." Nokomee did not smile, she only looked at me, and I saw there a deep loneliness, a tender need for companionship and sympathy that had never been filled in her life. She looked at me, and her lower lip trembled a little, her eyes suddenly averted from mine.

"Nokomee, there is so much we would have to tell each other, you of your life, and I of the great country of which you have never heard. Would you not like to see the great cities of my country?"

She shook her head, turned on me with sudden fierce words:

"When you came and struck down that hideous cross-eyed man, my heart went out to you in gratitude. Go, while my heart remains soft, it is not so often that the heart of a *Zerv* is soft toward any outlander. Go, I cannot protect you from this place."

"I will stay," I said.

"Stubborn fool!" She stamped her foot prettily, imperiously, vexed at my refusal to go out of that weird place the way I had entered. "Stay then, but do not expect me to keep off the slaves of the Goddess. This place can be most evil to those who do not know what it is, nor why it is secret."

She turned, walked behind the great dais of the crystal sarcophagus, and I followed just in time to see her disappear behind a hanging curtain of leather. I hastened after, my hand on my gun, for I had no wish to be left alone where I had seen my three companions stricken down with no enemy in sight.

Behind the curtain a passage led, along the passage were several doors. She sped past these lightly, almost running. I followed, she must have heard me, but she did not look back. The doors along the passage were curtained. Through the gaps of the curtain I could see they were empty of life. The curtains were rotted as if long unused, dirty and blotched with mould staining the leather.

Though she had spoken to me in Korean, and I had answered in the same tongue, I knew she was no native, for she spoke it differently, perhaps no better than myself. I was no judge; what she used may have been a dialect different from that I had heard previously.

I followed as she emerged from the long tunnel into the blaze of sunlight. She stood for a moment letting her eyes adjust to the glare. I stumbled to her side, half-blinded, stood looking down at the scene which seemed to engross her.

Gradually it came clear, like a television screen coming into perfect tune—the immense inner valley that the mountain of cloud-like snow enclosed. In the center of the encircled valley a lake shimmered blue as the sky, and about that lake was a city.

My eyes refused, at first, to accept what they were seeing. My mind rebelled, but after a minute of staring and making sure—I gasped.

Alien to this earth it was, but beautiful! Towers, and round-based dwellings braced together in one single unit of structural strength, a designed whole such as our architects dream of and never achieve. Walled with white marble, the city was a fortress, but a lovely fortress. Yet there was a coldness, an angularity, that told me these Zervs, as Nokomee had called her race, lacked true sympathy for life forms, lacked emotion as we know it in art. Yet it was beautiful, if repellent because so alien, so pure in design, so lacking in the sympathetic understanding of man's nature. This was a city no earthman could ever call home. It lacked something. There were no dogs, no strolling women or running children, it lay silent and waiting—for what?

Nokomee waved a hand.

"Titanis, our first earth colony. But it is no longer ours. The Schrees have taken it from us. That is why it is silent."

I did not understand. There were plodding lines of people, disciplined, carrying burdens, no bigger than ants at this distance. There was an ominous horror about the quiet beauty of the place. It was somehow like a beautiful woman lying just slain. Yet I could see no wounds of war, no reason for the feeling that I had, like the sudden shrinking one might have at sight of the stump of a man's arm just amputated.

I looked into Nokomee's face, and there were tears in her eyes. My heart sank. I felt a vast sympathy for her sorrow, though I could not understand.

"We planned so much with our new freedom here in your wilderness. Then came the raiders, to freeze our Queen in her sleep, to drive us into your forests, to make of us that remained mindless slaves and maimed horrors. I cannot bear it, stranger. I cannot…"

She turned and wept, her head on my chest. I patted her head, feeling entirely incompetent to console her for what injuries I could not imagine.

"What raiders, Nokomee? Tell me. Perhaps there is a way I can help. Who knows?"

"We are so few now, who were so many and so strong— and every day fewer. There is no hope. Do not try to wake it in me. It would be madness."

"Tell me. Perhaps that alone would help you."

"How can I tell you the long history of my home world, the immortal wisdom of our Queen, the strange science her immortal family gave her, of how we fought to protect her from our own tyrants and at last fled into space with her? How can I tell you of what she is? How could you understand the ages of struggle on our own world that reduced her kind to but a dozen, and left our kind, the mortals, at the mercy of the Schrees? You ask, but it is impossible for you to believe things you do not know about."

"Perhaps if I told you of my people and their life, you would understand that I could understand what you think is impossible for me. I am not ignorant as the others of earth people you have met. And my nation is numerous, the greatest of this earth."

"Our ways are too strange to you. But I will try. You need not try to tell me of your people; we examined your earth carefully before we chose this valley for our retreat. Here we built and raised the force wall to keep out inquiring interlopers like yourself who might bring the powers of your nation in ignorant war against us. But from our home world the Schrees were sent on our trail, and they found us. They were too many. Our only hope was in safe hiding, and they found us out. We did not know they could find us, or we would never have built. We thought pursuit had long been abandoned, but they are driven by single-minded hate, not by logic. It has been a lifetime of wandering they have followed us. It has been all my lifetime, making this home here, thinking ourselves safe—and then they came and destroyed all our work."

As she talked, she had quieted. We had resumed walking along the ledge of the mountainside. Suddenly from ahead a man leaped out, his strange weapon trained on my breast. I stood, not daring to move, while Nokomee shouted a string of shrill alien syllables at him. He thrust the weapon back in his belt, and fell in behind us as we passed. I could not help staring at him, and at the thing he had pointed at me.

It was a tapering tube about a foot long, triggered on the thumb side with a projecting stud, with a hand-grip shaped with finger grooves. I knew it was a weapon with a long history of development behind it by the simplicity of the lines, the entire efficiency of its appearance. The small end was a half-inch, perhaps, in bore, the big end perhaps three inches or less. He handled it as though it weighed but a trifle. I did not ask what it was.

The man himself was no taller than Nokomee, though much more solidly built, with thick, slightly bowed legs and heavy black brows on bulging bone structure, his eyes deep-set beneath. His ears, like Nokomee's, were high and too small to be natural. His teeth were larger than normal on earth, and the incisors smaller and more pointed, the canines heavier and longer. There was a point to his chin, heavy-angled and thick-boned as it was, it was not an earthman's chin. His neck was long, more supple and active, he kept moving his head in an unnatural watchfulness like a wild animal's. I wondered what other differences, small in themselves, but adding up to complete strangeness of aspect, I would find in time.

"That is Holaf," murmured Nokomee in Korean to me. "He is a chief among us now, since the fall of our strength. He is good, but young and always too impetuous. He needs long experience, and it looks as if he would get it, now."

"You have more than one leader?" I asked.

"We have three chiefs left to us, who rule their families—their clans. We have but one real leader. He is an old wise man left us by good fortune. He is our lone scientist. The chiefs of the clans listen to the leader, but they argue. Things look bad for us all."

"You are too few to reconquer the city?"

"Too few, yes. And time plays against us, for with the coming of the ships from our home planet—that I should call that tyrant's nest home!—there will be even more of the Schrees, then. We are a lost people now. There is no hope, eventually we will be hunted down as you earthmen will be hunted down, like animals. Made into slaves—and worse than slaves. You will learn what I mean when next you see your three friends."

It was too much for me. I asked:

"Why don't you leave this place, and go on to another?"

"On your little world? It is not big enough to hide ourselves from them. And we have lost our ships, we cannot get others."

"You think that they mean to conquer our whole planet?"

"In time they will do so. Not yet, but when they are many, they will spread, slaughter all who fight them, and enslave all who do not. They are very terrible creatures, not men at all, you know."

"Not like you and I?"

"Not at all. You will see, soon. Hurry, it is late, and we have council to attend."

There was a deep passion in her words, quick and sharp and strange on her lips as they were, a passion of anger and hopeless effort that somehow roused me into desire to help her and these strange people of hers. Too, if what she said was true, these raiders who had despoiled her people would in time engulf the world with a war of conquest, even if they were less able to defeat us than she estimated. I resolved to make the most of this opportunity to learn the worst of this hidden threat to men everywhere. I felt a kinship with Nokomee and her friend, silent and alert beside me, and I realized it could well be that I had in my hands the future of mankind, and that it behooved me not to let it fall through carelessness.

Lapsed now into silence, we reached the end of the trail along the ledge. We came out upon a broad shelf, with several cave mouths opening along its cliff-side. Gathered here in the twilight were some two-score men and women, bearing weapons; some the short powerful bow I had seen in Nokomee's hands; others weapons like Holaf's tapered tube; still others bearing small, round metal shields embossed with weird designs that meant nothing to me. Squatted here, without fire, they fell silent at our approach, eyeing me with curiosity and the beginnings of anger at my intrusion. Nokomee began to talk swiftly in that rattling, high-pitched tongue of theirs. I squatted down on my heels, took out my pipe, lit it. At the flare of my match Holaf struck it from my hand. I realized it had been a blunder, even a spark might attract attention to their presence on the hillside. Still, the incident told me Nokomee had not been lying to me.

Holaf pointed at the city far below, now glowing here and there with lights, and at the match on the ground. Then he motioned to a cave mouth, and I followed him. Inside there was a fire burning, furs strewn about the floor, metal urns and even mirrors hung on the rough stone walls. I sat on a rude wooden bench of newly-hewed wood, lit my pipe again without interference. But I was sorry to miss that conference outside in the open air. I wanted to hear, even if I could not understand. Holaf still remained by my side, and his hand did not leave the oddly-carved butt of the tapered tube-gun.

I sat there, feeling very much alone, with Holaf watching me somberly, the only light a flickering amber from the fire. I started to my feet as a musically pitched, almost singing voice questioned Holaf in their tongue. I looked about for the source, then saw her moving toward me in the half-light, and I stepped back in a kind of awe and embarrassment, for this was new.

She was as tall as myself, shaped with slender Amazonian strength, but curved and soft and subtly aware of her feminine allure, strongly interested and pleased at the awe and pleasure in my face. Her, rounded, fully adult body was sketched over with a web of silkily gleaming black net, light and unsubstantial as a dream, clinging and wholly revealing. Her eyes were dark-lidded and wide-set, her brow high and proud, and about her neck hung a web of emeralds set in a golden mesh of yielding links.

She came on, moving on shoes like Japanese water shoes, completely mystifying as to how she balanced on the stilt-like soles. Stepping thus in little balancing steps like a dancer, she moved very close, peering into my eyes, so that I blushed deeply at the nearness and the nudity of her, and she laughed, amusedly, as at a child. Her long, gemmed hand reached out and touched me, and she talked to Holaf excitedly, her face all smiles and interest; I was a wholly fascinating new toy he had brought her, it seemed. Then she sank to the bench, crossing her lovely knees over her hands, clasped together as if to make sure they behaved. To me she was wholly cultured and I some strange boor who had never been in a drawing room. I felt the impact of that culture in her interested eyes and in the sleek, smart bearing of her utterly relaxed body. She stretched a hand to gesture me to be seated, and I tried Korean on her.

"It is a pleasure to meet you, lady. If I but knew who you were, and how to speak properly, there is much we could find of interest to discuss."

"I am sure of it, stranger. First you must tell me of yourself, and then later we will talk of what is familiar to me. I cannot put off the curiosity which burns me. Please tell me all about your people and yourself!" Her voice was hard to follow, she handled the clumsy Korean with a bird-like quickness and an utter disregard for the nature of the language. Her eyes burned into my own, and I sat embarrassed beside her, tongue-tied, while Holaf smiled quietly and kept his hand on his weapon.

So I talked about New York, about my home town in Indiana, about my mine in South America, about anything and everything, and she listened, rapt eyes encouraging me, hanging on every stumbling, mispronounced, difficult word. I would have given an arm to have been able to talk expertly in her own tongue.

Thus engaged, and engrossed by her, I glanced up absently to note Nokomee's eyes blazing into my own in fury, and spaced about the room in a listening circle, a score of others. I stopped abruptly, and Nokomee lashed out at the woman beside me with a string of alien expletives that made her face flame with an anger as great as Nokomee's own. I wondered vaguely what I had done...

Their strange, grim faces, all watching me, seeming to peer inside me, trying to gauge me as an enemy or a friend. I stood up, for the exciting near-nude body of the woman who had caused Nokomee's outburst was too close, too intimately relaxed.

Abruptly Nokomee took me by the hand, led me out and along the ledge on the cliff. Into another cavern entrance she led me, to a smaller chamber, where another fire burned, and another bench invited to its warmth. She half pushed me to a seat, and busied herself in the next adjoining chamber, rattling dishware, and now and again giving a sharp exclamation as of extreme disgust.

I gathered I had been guilty of falling for the Zerv equivalent of a vamp. How wrong I was in this deduction I was to learn. It was not the woman's beauty that Nokomee feared, but something vastly more dangerous. I was very ignorant then. The Zervs were an ancient people and their ways were strange entirely. For the net-clad beauty had been a "Zoorph." I asked Nokomee, as she repeated the word again.

"What is a Zoorph, that makes you so angry? I thought she was very charming. I saw no harm in talking to her!"

Nokomee thrust her head out of the curtained doorway, from which the smell of food told me I had not eaten since morning.

"A Zoorph dear *child* of earth, is a creature not good for man or beast! Only a Zerv would be fool enough to keep so dangerous an animal about! If I told you, you would not believe it."

"Tell me anyway, Nokomee."

The girl came, bearing food on a tray. She squatted at my feet, putting the tray on the bench, and holding a large graceful urn of some liquid to replenish my cup. Very prettily she did this, yet I gathered that it was something which would have overwhelmed me with the honor if I had understood. I did appreciate her service, and I tried to say so, but she silenced me.

"Never mind, one day you will understand how proud we are, that in our own world and in our own society *you* would be less than a worm. Yet I serve you, who am more above you than a princess would be in your world. Thus does the world change about one, and one adjusts. But do not think of it. It must be, or some terrible thing like the Zoorph would seize upon you here among us."

I laughed a little, for I was sure she was telling a lie, to warn me against the "vamp" in the only words she could think of in the alien tongue.

Her face flushed deep red at my laughter, and she half rose as if to leave, but restrained her anger.

"A Zoorph is worse than a disease, it has enervated my people until they have lost everything, and still they are among us. They are children raised by a secret cult on my own world, trained into strange practices. It is somewhat like a witch or sorcerer would be to you, but much, much different. You could not understand unless you were raised among us. When men are tired of life, they go to a Zoorph. It is not nice to speak of, what they are and what they do. To us, it is like death, only worse. Yet we have them, as ants have pets, as dogs have lice, as your people have disease. It is a custom. It is a kind of escape from life and life's dullness— but it is escape into madness, for the Zoorph has an art that is utter degradation, and few realize how bad they are for us. You must never go near her again!"

Days passed into weeks, and every day I learned a few words of the Zerv language, every day I picked up a little more insight into their utterly different ways and customs and standards—their scale of values. It was a process replete with surprises, with revelations, with new understanding of nature itself as seen through the alien eyes.

I remained as a kind of semi-prisoner, tolerated because of Nokomee's position and her affection for me. Nokomee, I learned, was "of the blood," though there were few surviving of her family to carry on the power and prestige she would have inherited. Yet, she was "of the blood" and entitled to all the respect and obedience the Zervs gave even to their old ruler.

He was an attenuated skeleton of a man, with weary eyes and trembling hands, and I grew more and more sure that the inactivity against their usurpers visible in the valley beneath was due more to his age and timorous nature than to any inability to turn the tables. They seemed to hold the "Schrees" in contempt, yet never took any action against them, so that I wondered if the contempt were justified or was an inherited, sublimated hatred.

The supplies, rifles and ammunition which had been left on our horses when we entered the cavern of the golden image, had been brought to Nokomee's cavern and locked in a small chamber before my eyes. It was all there. As the time dragged on, I chafed at the inactivity, fought against the barriers of language and alien custom that separated me from these people, struggled to overcome their indifference and their, to me, impossible waiting for *what* I did not understand.

Finally I could wait no longer. In the night, I burst the lock of the closet with a bar, took out a rifle and .45 and two belts of cartridges. I slid over the lip of the ledge that hid us from the city's eyes. I was going to see for myself what we were hiding from, what we were waiting for, was going to take my chances with the dangers in that place they had built and from which they now hid. I had pressed Nokomee for explanations and promises of future participation in their life and activities, and I had been refused for the last time! Like a runaway, I slid down the steep cliff face, putting as much space between the Zervs and myself as rapidly as I could.

The night was dark as pitch. I had left Nokomee asleep in her chamber. I had avoided Holaf, who still kept a kind of amused watch over my activities, and I was free. Free to explore that weird city of plodding lives, of strange unexplained sounds, of ominously hidden activity!

Scrambling, sliding, worrying in the dimness, I finally reached the less precipitous slopes of the base of the cliff. As I stopped to get a bearing on the direction of the city, above me came a slithering, a soft feminine exclamation, and down upon me came a perfumed weight, knocking me sprawling in the grass.

My eyes quickly adjusted, I crawled to the dim shape struggling to her feet. Her face was not Nokomee's, as I had at first thought. Those enormous shadowed eyes, that thin lovely nose, the flower-fragile lips, the mysterious allure— were the woman whom Nokomee had described as a "Zoorph" and whom she had both feared and despised. I spoke sharply in the tongue of the Zervs. I had learned enough under Nokomee's tutelage to carry on a conversation.

"Why do you follow me, Zoorph?"

"Because I am weary of being cooped up with those who do not trust me, just as you. I want to find a new, exciting thing; just as do you. Even if it is death or worse, I want it. I am alive, as are you."

I put down the dislike and distrust the girl Nokomee had aroused in me against her. Perhaps she *had* been merely jealous of her.

"Don't you *know* what could happen in the city?" To me it was curious that she should want to go where the others feared to go.

"I know no better than you what awaits there, and I do not believe what they have told me of the Schrees. They are not wholly human, but neither are they evil wholly, as the Zervs suppose."

"Why do the Zervs wait, instead of trying to do something for themselves? They speak of the threat of these raiders, yet they do not try to help me bring others of my people here to stop the threat they speak of so fearfully. I do not understand."

"The old ruler thinks the ships will come and drive them off from his city. But he is wrong, they will never come. It is like waiting for the moon to fall. The raiders' ships will return, and they will be stronger than ever. But not a ship of the Zervs remains in neighboring space to succor us. Yet he hopes, and his followers wait. It is foolish, and he cannot trust you or men like you to get help for him. He is too old to meet new conditions and to understand."

Few of the Zervs had shown the rapt interest in me and my people that this Zoorph had made so plain. I thought backward on how carefully she and I had been kept apart since our first meeting, and I realized there was more to it than Nokomee's words of anger.

"What is a Zoorph, and what is your name? Why did Nokomee warn me against all Zoorphs?"

"A Zoorph is a member of a cult; a student of mysteries not understood by the many. The others have a superstition about us, that we destroy souls and make others slaves to our will. It is stupid, but it is like all superstitions—hard to disprove because so vague in nature." She flickered impossible eyelashes at me languishingly, in perfect coquetry. "You don't think me dangerous to your soul, do you?"

I didn't. I thought her a very charming and talented woman, whom I wanted to know much better. I said so, and she laughed.

"You are wiser than I thought, to see through their lies. They are good people, but like all people everywhere, they have their little insanities, their beliefs and their intolerances."

Yet within me there was a little warning shudder borne of the strange power of her eyes on my own, of the chill of the night, of many little past-observed strangenesses in her ways, in the fear the Zervs bore for her. I reserved something of caution. She saw this in my eyes and smiled sadly, and that sad and understanding smile was perfectly calculated to dispel my last doubt of her. I slid closer across the grass, to lie beside her.

"What could I gain by a knowledge of what lies in the city, Zoorph?" I asked.

"My name is *Carna*, stranger. In that city you can learn whether there is danger for your people in what the Schrees plan on earth. We could not tell that, for we do not know enough about your own race's abilities. You could steal a vehicle to take you to your own rich cities. And as for me, I could go with you, to practice my arts in your cities and become rich and famous."

"What are your arts, Carna?"

"Nothing you would call spectacular, perhaps. I can read thought, I can foretell the future, and I can sometimes make things happen fortunately, if I try very hard. Such things, very unsubstantial arts, not like your gun which kills. Subtle things, like making men fall in love with me, perhaps."

She laughed into my eyes and I got abruptly to my feet. She was telling the truth in the last sentence, and I did not blame Nokomee for fearing her power.

"Let us see, then, Carna, what the night can give us. I cannot wait forever for chance to bring me freedom. Come," I bent and helped her to her feet, very pleasant and clinging her grasp on my arm, very soft and utterly smooth the flesh of her arm in my hand, very graceful and lovely her swift movement to rise. My heart was beating wildly, she was a kind I understood, but could not resist any the better for knowing. Or was I unkind, and she but starved for kindness and human sympathy, so long among a people who disliked and feared her?

We walked along in the darkness, the distant moving lights of that city closer each step, and a dread in my breast at what I would find there, a dread that grew. Beside me Carna was silent, her face lovely and glowing in the night, her step graceful as a deer's.

We circled the high wall of white marble keeping some twenty feet away, where the grass gave knee-high cover we could drop into instantly. We came around to the far side from the cliff, and stopped where a paved highway ran smooth, like pebbled glass, straight across the valley. I glanced at Carna, she gestured toward the open gate in the wall, and smiled a daring word.

"In…?"

"In!" I answered, and like two kids, hand in hand, we stole through the shadowed gateway, sliding quickly out of the light, standing with our backs to the wall, looking up the long, dim-lit way along which a myriad dark doorways told of life. But it was seemingly deserted. Carna whispered softly:

"When it was ours, the night was gay with life and love, now—*it is death!*"

"Death or taxes, we're going to take a look."

We stole along the shadowed side of the street, the moon was up, shedding much too bright a light now for comfort. Perhaps a hundred yards along that strange street we went, I letting the Zoorph lead the way, for I had an idea she must know the city and have some plan, or she would not be here. If she meant to use me to escape into my world, I was all for her.

Then, from ahead, came the sound of feet, many of them in unison. We darted into a doorway, crouched behind a balustrade. Nearer came the feet, and I peered between the interstices of the screening balustrade. The feet came on; slow, rhythmic, marching without zest or pause or break, perfection without snap. As the first marching figure came into sight in the moonlight, I shuddered to the core with something worse than fear.

For they were men who were no longer men! When Barto and Polter and Noldi had been carried off unconscious, Nokomee had told me:

"They are not my people. They go their way and we go ours. Time has made us a people divided. Time, *and a cruel science*."

These were the mole-men, the crab-men, the creatures built for specific purposes as tools are built. Each *thing* bore on his back a bale of goods, or a bar of metal, a burden sizeable enough for two ordinary men. They were strong, and they were silent and smooth-moving as machines. I realized they *were* machines—made out of flesh.

"Are these slaves, or what?" I asked Carna.

"These were once the slaves, or workmen of the race of Zervs. They now serve the Schrees, for they are mindless, in a way. They are not important. It is those who guard and guide them I wait to see. I have not yet seen a Schree, but only heard the Zervs describe them."

The nightmare procession went on for minutes, long minutes that were to me a nightmare. Yet I realized that if I had been raised to the idea of humankind made into machines, it would not be revolting—not after they had been hereditarily moulded for centuries into what they were. Yet what a crime it was, what they might have been if left to develop as nature intended, rather than as man cruelly mal-intended. They must have been once specially selected for strength as well as beauty, for about them was a sad and terrible grace, a remainder of noble chiseling of brow and nostril, distorted as by a fiend into the horror that it was— these had once been a noble race!

"Do you feel the terrible horror of this sight?" I asked Carna.

"Always I have felt the horror that was done to them in the past. It is *still* done to man. Look, there are the three who came with you, and fell into the hands *of the priests*. They are the thing that the Zervs *really fear*, yet they live with it, and have done so for centuries. They can despise the Schrees, but they are as bad themselves—look!"

I followed with my eye her pointing finger. Yes, that figure *was* hulking Barto, and I almost yelled "Jake, snap out of it!" before I remembered my own peril.

Then he came into the full light, and passed not twenty feet away. I leaned against the railing of stone, sick as a dog and retching. They had made him over, with some unknown aborted science of an evil world! Jake was clubfooted, lumbering, with his jaws grown into great jowls of bone, his arms elongated and ending in hooks. Two of the fingers, or the thumb and finger had been enlarged or grafted into a bone-like semblance of a crab's claw. What he was going to be when they got through, I didn't know, but neither did Jake. He didn't know anything! He clumped along, his crossed eyes unmoving, his back bent with a weight heavy for even his broad shoulders—a man no longer, but a mindless zombie. A cross-eyed zombie!

I cursed silently, tearing my hands against the stone as I resisted the impulse to fire and fire again upon those hopping, thin, white things that came after.

"Just *what* are those hopping things?"

"They are a separate race, who have lived with both Zervs and with Schrees. They are a part of our life. You have dogs, horses, machines. We have *Jivros*—that is, priests—and we have the workmen we call Shinros, and too, we have the Zoorphs!" She laughed a little as I stared at her. "Do not worry, the Zoorphs are not really so different. But the Schrees and Shinros *are* different."

"Damned, beastly, demoniac life it must be."

"To you, who expect things to be like your knowledge tells you it must be. To us, it is our way. For a Zerv, or for a Schree, it is a good way. The Jivros do the supervisory work, the Shinros do the hard work, and the Schrees take it easy and enjoy life. Why do you have machines?"

"Machines are not alive. That is different."

"Neither are the Shinros alive, they only seem so. They do not know what they have lost—it is much as if they had died.

"But come, I must show you where we can get a ship to take us away from this and into your world. I have a life to live, I want to *live* it! You—have a message to deliver to your people, or they will become the Shinros of the whole race of Schrees. I do not like to think what can happen to your world!"

I followed her again on our furtive way among the shadows. She was swift and sure, and made good time. She knew where she was going. It was a broad open space deep within the city. On three sides were wide closed doors like hangar doors. The fourth was a massive structure of rose granite, beetling above us, a monstrous shape in the dimness, throwing a shadow half across the paved space. We raced across the shadow toward the nearest doorway, flattened against it, listening for life inside. Carna worked on the catch of the door, after a second slid the door aside slowly, carefully. Inside I could see a shimmering smoothness, round, higher than my head, a top-shaped object. I guessed that this was the ship she meant to steal from the Schrees. Suddenly the door she was sliding open scraped, and emitted a shrill, high-pitched sound. I did not know if it was an alarm activated by the opening door or just rust on the rails and wheels of the door mechanism. Carna cried:

"Hurry, get into the ship, we must take off at once. They will come; they must have heard that sound!"

I ducked into the darkness, circled the bulging shape, looking for an opening. Smooth, there seemed no way I could find.

"Here it is, help me open it," Carna panted behind me.

I leaped to her side. She was twisting at an inset handle around which faint lines indicated the door edge. I pulled her aside, took hold of the handle, twisted hard. It bent, then gave, and the door swung easily open in my hands. We tumbled in. Carna raced through the first chamber, and even as I got the door closed, the floor lifted under my feet easily, drifted out of the wide doorway, shot upward so quickly I was thrown to the floor. I lay there, the increasing acceleration pressing me hard against the cool metal. After a time I struggled up, made my way to the woman's side.

Ahead was the moonlit range of mountains. Carna was setting a course straight along the ridge of them, heading southward.

"How far will this thing fly?" I asked.

"It will fly around your world many times, if I want it to."

"What kind of fuel does it use?" I asked incredulously.

"I don't know what that is. It uses a substance we call Ziss. It is a good fuel."

"It must be!"

I looked back along the ridge of the mountain's top toward the valley we had left. We were in a bubble on the top of the flat, circular ship; one could see in any direction. Back there a series of glowing round shapes shot upward, came after us in a long curve that would bring them ahead of us on our course. Carna changed her course to parallel the pursuit, and they changed again, to intercept her new direction. Again she changed, circling farther west.

But it was no use! Rapidly they overhauled us.

"Can't you get more speed out of it?" I shouted at her, for they were very close.

"We have been unlucky, my friend. This ship is not in good shape. There is something wrong with it. I cannot make it go as it should, or there is something I do not know…"

Swiftly they came up with us, over us, and beams of light shot from them down upon us. The ship was held now, rigid. One could feel the acceleration cease. Like a bird on a string we followed as they swung back toward the valley. Minutes later we were being lowered into the open space we had just left. I clicked the safety off my rifle, loosened the gun in my holster. I covered the door, shielding myself behind the round shape of a machine. But Carna put a hand on my weapon, shook her head.

"If you kill some of them, they will make of you a Shinro. If you submit meekly, it may be I can talk to someone and save you. I have ways. I understand them. They will be glad to get me, and I will tell them *you* know many things they need to know. I can save your life. Later we can try again, in another ship. Next time we will not be so unlucky."

It sounded like sense, and I looked into her deep eyes searchingly. She meant well. Perhaps she could do what she said. I did not know these aliens; she was almost one of them.

As the door opened in the side, I lay the rifle down, stood with crossed arms as the thin, hopping horrors came near.

These things had *never* been men. They had faces that were empty of features, just flat, shiny, gray eyes, two holes where they breathed, no mouth that I could see. There was a long neck around which the collar of their white robe was gathered in folds. Their hands were horny, like an insect's claws. They were not human, they were only four-limbed, and walked—or hopped—in an erect position. There the resemblance ceased.

They led us out, Carna rattling off a series of sounds I could hardly follow. Something about:

"We had to flee from the Zervs, we did not believe you would take us in, we had to steal a ship. I am Carna, a Zoorph of the first grade, and this man is a native of the United States, the greatest country of this earth. Do not harm him, he can help you if he wishes."

Her words must have had quite an effect, for the weird, insect-like men examined me with their eyes as we hurried along, across the hangar space, into the big building of rose granite. Within twenty minutes we were entering a tremendous room, and Carna nudged me.

"Their boss, Carl! Look impressed."

It was easy to look impressed. I *was* mightily impressed by the *She* on the throne!

I had no eyes for the score or so of Schrees that surrounded the massive carved chair, even though I was curious about their difference from men. Above them were her sleepy eyes, wide almonds, molten and wise, incandescent with intense inner fire above a mouth that was a wide, scarlet oval torn into the whitely-glowing face.

A great black pelt softened the harsh lines of the throne, framed her chalk-white body so that it curved starkly sensual, dominating the great chamber with beauty. It was a beauty one knew this woman used as a tool, a weapon, keen and polished and ready, and it struck at me swift as a great serpent, the fires behind her eyes driving the blow.

She wore a kind of sark of shadowy black veil, sewn over with sparkling bits of gem. It was in truth but an effective ornament for the proud firm breasts, the narrow waist, the arch of the hips and the curves of her thighs. Inadvertently I let out a low whistle of approbation and astonishment. Carna, beside me, nudged me sharply, and I snapped out of it.

The purple, lazy lids of her eyes moved, the slow weary-wise gaze centered on me, her hand moved. In two strides a man from the throne-side had me by the arm, and another seized my other, tugged me forward to her feet, thrust me down on my knees. Still, I looked. Curiosity and something more held me in a grip I couldn't shake.

This was more than a woman, I sensed. There was an awe of her throbbing in me. Not fear—something deeper, something one feels before the unexplainable, something one feels gazing at the moon and wondering; an ominous, deep, thrilling and unexplainable emotion.

Closer, I could see her firm flesh was dusted over with a glittering powder, the soft curves of her hair swept back to mingle and lose themselves in the black fur of the pelt so that the night-black hair seemed to spread everywhere about her and melt into the shadows.

Her hands were sinuous as serpents, the fingers tapering, the nails very long like the Chinese. Her nose was exquisite, but thin-edged, and with a cruel line on each side that vanished when she spoke.

"It is death to strangers in this valley..." she mused, not speaking to me or to anyone, but with a cruel intent to toy with me in the words, mocking, waiting for me to answer.

"I have been long on the way," I answered, in much the same tone, as though we were speaking of some one not present.

"The way to death is sometimes long, and sometimes short. And, too, there are things worse than death. But what was it you came here seeking?"

"I did not know, until just now," I answered, still looking at her eyes, which glanced at me, then away, then back again.

She was interested in spite of her apparent weariness with routine—or perhaps with life itself.

"Now that you know, will you tell me?" She smiled a little, not a good smile, but a secret jest with herself. An appearance of extreme evil sat for a moment on her face, then went again, like the wind. Her voice was grave, careless, yet modulated with an extreme care as if she spoke to a child.

"I seek the wisdom I see in your eyes, to know what is and why it wearies you. I want to know a great many things, about your people and what they do here, what they mean to mine, what your plans may be—a great many things I need now."

The sleepiness left her eyes, and she bent toward me with the grace of a great cat and the shadows circling her eyes lifted a little. Wise, aloof, indifferent, yet she did not know what I was, or what I meant, and she meant to find out.

"So you know…" she mused, as if to herself.

"I know you are from space. I know it has been a long long time since you first touched here; your people, that is. I know that you drove the Zervs from this city and took it for your own. But that is all."

"It is too much. You cannot leave here." Her voice was sharp, and I was surprised to learn that she had even considered letting me go free. It was encouraging, after the dire pictures the Zervs and Nokomee had drawn for me of these Schrees.

I looked curiously at them, the Zervs had called them "not human." They *were* different, as a negro is different from a white, or an Oriental from a Finn. Their eyes were wide-set and a little prominent, their ears thinner and smaller, their necks very long and supple—different still from the Zervs. Yet they were a human race. I had misunderstood—or I had not yet met those whom the Zervs called Schree.

Carna had knelt beside me, and I murmured to her:

"Are these the Schrees, or something else?"

"These are the high-class Schrees, they are very like the Zervs in appearance. The other classes of the Schrees at sometime in the past were changed by medical treatments into a different appearance. It was a way of fixing the caste system permanently—understand?" She answered me swiftly, in a whisper, and the woman on the throne frowned as she noticed our conversation.

Her eyes fixed ours as she said, with a curiously excited inflection, no longer bored with us: "Take these two to the place of questioning. I will supervise the proceeding. I must know what these two intended here, whether others of this man's people understand us."

"We're in for it!" said Carna, and I knew what she meant. Jerked to our feet, we were hurried from the big throne room, down a corridor, through a great open door which closed behind us.

That place! It was a laboratory out of Mr. Hyde's nightmares.

Up until now I had accepted the many divergencies and peculiarities of the Zervs, the priestly insect-men, the monstrous workers—all the variance of this colony from space—as only to be expected of another planet's races. I had consciously tried to resist the impact of horror on my mind, had tried to put it aside as a natural reaction and one which did not necessarily mean that this expedition from space was a horrible threat to men. I had tried to accept their ways as not necessarily monstrous, but as a different way of life that *could* be as good a way as our own if I once understood it. There were attractive points about the Zervs and even about these Schrees' rulers which bore out this impulse toward tolerance in me.

But in this laboratory—or *abattoir*—some nameless, ominous aura or smell or electric force—what it was I know not—struck at my already staggering understanding with a final blow.

Now at last I met the real Schrees! I knew without asking. They seemed to me to be an attempt by the peculiar insect-like "priests" to make from normal men a creature more like themselves in appearance. Perhaps it had been done from the natural urge to have about them beings more like themselves than men…and it was plain that the race of the insect-like creatures and of men had become inextricably linked—become a social unity in the past. It was also increasingly plain that the four-limbed insect creatures had in the beginning been the cultured race, been the fathers of the science and culture of this race, had through the centuries lost their dominance to the Zervs and the Schree's upper classes—had retained the "priest" role as their own place in society. It was perhaps at that time that their science had brought the Schree type into existence. There were perhaps a hundred of them at work in the big chamber—a chamber bewilderingly filled with hanging surgical non-glare lights, filling the place with a shadowless illumination, revealing great, gurgling bottles of fluid with tubes and gleaming metal rods; pulsing elastic bulbs; throbbing little pumps, with row on row of gauges and dials and little levers along the walls.

There were a score of ominous-looking operating tables, some occupied, some empty, about them gathered group after group of white-masked Schrees. These were taller than men, near seven feet, with very bony arms and legs, a skeletal structure altered into attenuation, with high, narrow skulls, great liquid eyes, no brows, hairless skulls showing bare and pointed above the white surgical masks.

Very like the Jivro caste, yes, but different as men are different from insect. They walked with a long graceful stride, not hopping as the priests' class. Their eyes were mournful and liquid with a dog-like softness, their hands were snake-quick and long, they looked like sad-faced ghouls busy about the dismemberment of a corpse—a corpse of someone they had loved, and they appearing very sad about the necessity. Such was their appearance; mournful, ghoulish, yet human and warm in a repressed, frustrated way.

The tall, sad-eyed Schrees turned from the preparation of two rigs like dental chairs, except that they were not that at all, but only similarly surrounded with gadgetry incomprehensible to me. We had stood isolated, waiting, with four guards between us and the door.

As we were each placed in one of these chairs, our wrists and ankles fastened with straps of metal, I expected almost any horrible torture to be inflicted upon us.

They shot a beam of energy through my head and I heard words, sentences, a rapid expounding of alien grammar and pronunciation which sank deep into my brain. My memory was being ineradicably written upon with all the power needed to make of me whatever they wanted. But apparently their only purpose now was to give me a complete understanding of their language. An hour, two, swept by, and now the heretofore almost unintelligible gibberish about me became to my ears distinct and understandable words. I was now acquainted with the tongue of the Schrees, far better than little Nokomee had taught me the somewhat different tongue of the Zervs.

Then they wrapped about my waist and chest a strong net of metal mesh, and I knew that now something strenuous was going to occur, for I could not move a muscle because of the complete wrapping of metal mesh.

Now a metal disk was set to swinging in front of my nose so that I could not see what they were doing to my companion. I watched the metal disk, and saw behind it the tall swaying figure of the Queen enter and approach. She stopped a few feet from my chair, and her eyes were intent upon me. Then a light flashed blindingly in the reflecting disk, it went back and forth faster and faster, and I felt a strong vibration of energy pass in a beam through my head, throbbing, throbbing…darkness engulfed me. It was a darkness that was a black whirlwind of emotion. The sense of the desertion by humankind, by God and mercy and rationality swept through me and overwhelmed my inner self. I will never forget the utter agony of shrieking pain and loss that formed a whirling ocean of darkness into which I dived…

In this maelstrom of seeming destruction I lost all grip, had no will, was at sea mentally. Into this shrieking hurricane of madness a calm voice intruded. I recognized a familiar note—it was the ruler herself, her voice no longer bored, but with a cruel curiosity that I knew meant to be satisfied if it killed me.

"Tell me what your people intend to do about the flying saucers they speak of in their newspapers?"

"They do not believe they exist; they are told they are delusions," I heard myself answering. I was surprised to hear my voice, for it came with no conscious volition on my part.

"That is for the public; that is a lie. But what do the powers behind the scenes intend to do about them?"

"They are searching for them, to learn all they can about them. They do not understand where they come from, but they have some information. They suspect they are from space, and are afraid of them."

"And they sent you here to learn what you could. They brought you the golden statuette to help you gain an entry, did they not?"

I tried to resist the impulse to tell the truth, for I could realize that if she thought I had the power of my government behind me, my fate might be different than if I did not. I tried to say "yes, they sent me," but I could not! I answered like an automaton:

"No, my government has no knowledge of my expedition. I came purely to get gold and for no other reason. Mining is my business."

She gave a little exclamation of frustration. Then after a pause she asked:

"Do you think our way of life and your own could live together in peace, could grow to be one?"

Again I made futile efforts to hide my revulsion and fear of them all. It was no use. The flood of force pouring through my head was more effective than any truth serum.

"No, to me you are horrors, and my people would never consent to live at peace with you. You could never conquer us. Until the last of our cultured members were dead they would resist the horrible practices of your culture."

"That is as I surmised," she mused. "But I would have you tell me why this is so. What is it you find so revolting about us."

"What have you done to my companions? Do you think men want that to happen to them?"

"That was a punishment for entering here without permission. That would not happen to any but enemies."

"Men could never accept the altering of the shapes of workers, the tinkering with the hereditary form of their children, the artificial grafting upon our race of revolting and unnecessary form changes. Your whole science is a degeneration of wisdom into evil, tampering with life itself. You are horrors, and you do not know it."

I could hear her steps as she turned and left, tapping angrily upon the floor. After her I could hear the shuffling, heavier tread of her retinue. As the flood of vibration ceased, I began to curse aloud for the undiplomatic truths I had been forced to utter. In seconds my arms were free, and I was led out, a tall grim-faced guard on each side, with a firm grip on my arms. I wondered what was happening to the lovely Zoorph, but I did not get a chance to look. I was thrown into a cell, and the heavy wooden door shut. The thud of a bar dropped in place punctuated the evening's experience with a glum finality.

I lay for hours with my mind in a whirl from the effects of the truth ray. Jivros, or insect-priests, moved phantom-like before my sleepless eyes, watching from the dark and waiting. Gradually my thinking became more normal, and I began a systematic analysis and summing up of what I had learned of these people. There were but a few members of the ruling groups, and it was evident the rule was split between the Jivro caste of the insect men and some normal-appearing groups who had divided the power with them in the past. Under these were the Schrees, and under these the malformed working caste or castes. The Schrees had contact with some space-state, the Zervs were outcasts of the ruler caste who had been driven from that space-state—perhaps more than one planet—sometime in the past and had hid out upon earth until recently located by the power that ruled on their home planets. Now they were fugitive and nearly powerless, and I knew the Zervs were few in number from my own observation. There were perhaps a hundred, perhaps two hundred. They had contact with some of the Jivros with whom they were familiar, but the appearance of Jake and Noldi and Polter among the workmen in the city told me that these Jivros could be traitors to them, could be giving new allegiance to the conquerors of the Zervs. My mind centered on two facts. The Jivro caste were the real source of the evil in these people. It was their unnatural attitude toward human life which had made this race the horror it was, and they were still exercising that evil influence.

Morning came through a high barred window, and after a while food came, slid beneath the door. I did not see the bearer of the food, though I called out in curiosity. He did not answer, only shuffled wearily away.

The morning crawled past, the sun mounted until I could see the golden orb near zenith. Then came what I dreaded, the tread of a number of feet. The bar was lifted; I saw four armed guards and a waiting white-robed Jivro, his protruding pupiless eyes moving as he ran his gaze over my figure. I could not help shrinking from the horror of his examination, brief though it was, for I realized he might be deciding just what freak of nature he could make out of me.

I was marched out, down the corridor, up a long ramp, a turn, along two other corridors, up another ramp. The tour ended before a wide metal door, the guards spaced themselves at each side, the door was opened by the agile, hopping Jivro. I went in ahead of it.

There were but four beings in the room, and I stood before the long, foot-high table behind which the four reclined upon cushioned couches.

They were four divergent creatures. One was the queen, whose name I had yet to hear spoken. One was a very old Jivro, his skin ash-white and covered with a repulsive scale, like leprosy. The third was a mournful-eyed Schree, clad in an ornamented smock-like garment, from which his thin limbs thrust grotesquely. The fourth was a handsome, long-necked male who resembled the queen. He lounged negligently some distance from the three, as if in attendance upon her. I deduced he was her paramour, husband or close relative, perhaps a brother.

I stood eyeing them silently, waiting. I gathered the three heads of the government were here, and the extra one represented the balance of power in the hands of the queen. His negligent lack of interest seemed to me to be an evident giving of his voice to the queen, if he was a part of this gathering.

The queen's voice had lost its sleepy, mocking tones, was sharp, incisive:

"You present a problem new to us, earthman. Sooner or later, if we decide to remain upon this planet permanently, we will have to meet and conquer, or meet and engage in commerce with the other members of your race. You are the first educated member of your race who has fallen into our hands. We must study your people, and we would like your willing cooperation. Will you give it willingly? Or must we put you to death? Which would perhaps symbolize, even indicate directly, our future attitude toward your races."

"I am quite willing," I said, before I had a chance to bungle it worse, "quite willing to exchange information on your people for the same about my own. However, I doubt that your people will find this planet congenial to an invader who ignores the natives as you have done."

"We did not come here to colonize, earthman. We came in pursuit of renegades from our law, fugitives who fled when their plots were uncovered. But we are considering the possibility of a permanent colony here, and you could help us..."

For an instant her eyes dwelt upon mine with a peculiar warning expression, as evident as a wink, and the expression was evanescent as a breath. I caught on, and made my face agreeable and subservient. Immediately her own reassumed a harsh, proud set, her voice became even more incisive and cold.

My eyes drifted casually to the blank, cold stare of the old Jivro, to the mournful liquid eyes of the Schree, on to the apparently disinterested gaze of the queen's friend. The only ominous feeling I got was from the eyes of the aged insect-man, and my deduction that they were the source of the evils of these people was strengthened. The chills ran down my back, and something within me thrilled as I understood that this queen was playing a part to please the Jivros, that her interests were actually divergent. Her voice was saying:

"You could help us greatly by explaining your life to us, who are so different; make it possible that in the future trade and cultural intercourse might spring up between the two alien ways of life. There will be no peace without understanding, you realize!"

"I quite agree with your views, and will help you in any way that I can," I said loudly, for the old Jivro seemed to be hearing with difficulty. He leaned back at my words, seemed to relax as if pleased.

The queen turned to her companion, smiled and said:

"Genner, you will see that he is taken care of as a guest, and endeavor to learn what you can from him. I will hold you responsible for the success of this experiment."

"Very well," Genner murmured, "but it seems to me, Wananda Highest, that we can never allow the wall of secrecy between ourselves and the people of this planet to be breached. To consider doing otherwise…" for an instant his eye hesitated upon hers, then he went on, "…could hardly be logical, but of course, there is much we could learn from them, and they from us. That, I see, as the only purpose of this exception."

Just then a great hullabaloo broke out in the corridors outside, the door burst open, and into the room three captives were borne, half-carried, half-pushed. I stood back out of the way, and the three were prodded into a row in front of the low table. Among them I recognized with a start my erstwhile guard, Holaf, of the Zervs.

Wananda leaned forward, her eyes glittering with sudden triumph, her voice thrilling with a cruel mocking note.

"More of the skulking Zervs fail to avoid our warriors! Where did you find them, Officer?"

"They were attempting to release the captive Croen female in the crystal prison of the cave of the Golden statue, your highness. Our spies among the Zervs informed us of the attempt."

Wananda's eyes blazed at Holaf. Her voice became more shrill with something almost like fear. The three men shrank back visibly from her fury.

"So it is not enough you plot treason, you must also turn against your Gods? You know the Croen powers, you know what she would do to us all, you included. But so that you can overcome the Schrees, nothing else to you is sacred, nothing too vile for you to do. Away with them, let them become the least among the mindless men."

The tall Schree warriors, their long faces expressionless, started to hustle the three captives toward the door again. Holaf wrenched free, turned, his face contorted with hatred.

"You have hounded us until we are but few, Wananda the Faithless, but you will never conquer us. We still have your doom in our hands, and it will find you out. Death to you, woman without mercy, creature without soul! These sacred Jivros plot your downfall, and your people pray that they will succeed. The ancient Jivro rule would be better than the justice you administer, you snake in a woman's flesh!"

The Schree holding Holaf's arms let go, tugged a weapon from his belt, struck Holaf over the head with it. He slumped unconscious, with blood running over his face from the blow. The three were taken out, and Wananda leaned back. Seeing my intent face, she waved a hand to her companion, Genner, who rose to his feet and motioning to me, preceded me from the room by another door than that which I had entered. I followed him.

Apparently I was on my honor, for no guard followed, and Genner bore no weapons I could see but a little jeweled dagger in his belt.

As he walked a step ahead of me, I asked:

"Who is this Croen that Holaf spoke of, in the crystal column. I saw her, wondered at her, in the room of the golden goddess. Why do they think she could be released?"

"The Croen are a powerful race of wizards, Carlin Keele. They live far off from our home planets in space, and they have a code of conduct that makes them monitors, doctors, interferers in all matters of other races' business. If she were released, she would at once attempt to overthrow our power, to set up a state after the Croen pattern. It is their way. They consider themselves as superior to all others, and they do have a knowledge of nature which they use to impose their will upon all peoples. They are worshipped as Gods by many primitive people, and so consider themselves above all laws but their own. She was captured many years ago in an attempt to overthrow the rule of Wananda upon a small satellite planet. Wananda did not kill her, but placed her in suspended animation within the protective crystal plastic. Our queen intends to revive her and study her mind for her wisdom, but we have not had time because of the press of events. Soon, now, she will become a tool in our hands to build greater the eminence of Wananda."

"Peculiar looking creature, yet attractive," I murmured.

"The Croens are physically beautiful, but they are warlike and cruel, they do not desire peace and the way of life of the Schrees and Jivros is an irritant to them. They hate and despise us, and we return them the favor."

I did not reply, but my heart seemed to throb in sympathy with the Zerv attempt to free the beautiful creature from her living tomb.

"Could she turn the tables for the Zervs if they had succeeded?"

"I really don't know," answered Genner, opening a door and motioning me into the apartment. "These are my quarters. There is plenty of room, the place is usually empty of all but slaves. I seldom sleep here myself, preferring more congenial and less lonesome sleeping accommodations. I think you will find it comfortable. I will see you at the evening meal time."

As I walked in, the door closed and I heard the lock click. I was a "guest" with reservations.

Curiously I examined the place, the unreadable books kept in niches behind transparent sections of the wall, the strange furnishings, at once exotic and comfortless to me. The books I could not get at, finding no way to open the transparent panels which seemed an integral part of the wall. I could not feel comfortable in the seats and lounges, as they were very low, requiring an oriental squat at which I am not adept. I compromised by stretching out along a hard couch raised some six inches above the floor. There were no gadgets to tinker with, the place was to me barren of necessary appurtenances...strange people, indeed.

As I was dozing off, the lock clicked in the door, and I sat up, startled to see Wananda glide in and close the door quickly behind her. She was alone, and there was something furtive about her.

"Welcome to my abode, beautiful one."

The woman smiled, an almost human smile; reserved, yet with an unexpected warmth. I waited with intense curiosity for her explanation of her visit.

"I come to you for aid, for I can talk to none of my own. I am in trouble which perhaps no one but you could remedy. Will you give me your honor, will you do what I ask without question, will you be my friend?"

I was taken aback that this apparently powerful personage should be seeking aid of me, a prisoner. I answered:

"I see no reason why you should not trust me, as I know no one here to betray you to. But are you not the supreme power here? Why should you want my aid?"

"Because you do not understand my position does not mean that I am not in trouble. These Jivros are difficult allies for one with blood in her veins. I was raised to be a ruler. The Jivro priests were my tutors and my administrators before I came of age. It is only reluctantly they have followed the orders from the rulers of our home planets to obey me. They intend to slay me, and report my death as an accident. I live in fear, and I have long awaited their treachery. There is but one hope for me and that is Cyane, the Superior One whom I saved only by enclosing her in that living coffin. That is what I ask of you—to succeed where the Zervs have failed, and to release her and guide her in flight from here. She can lead your people, save them from these monstrous Jivros who have made of my race the things which you see. I would save your people as well as myself. Will you try to release her?"

I leaned back against the cushions, crossed my legs, took out my pipe. This was not exactly a surprise, but I had not realized the rift between her and the peculiar insect-men was such as to cause her to fear for her life.

"How does one release a person from such a death?" I asked. "In my people's understanding of life, death comes with the stopping of the breath."

"She can be released by an injection of a stimulant which I can obtain for you. She is not dead, but in a condition very near to death, like a spider stung by a wasp. If she were free, she would soon scour your earth clean of the Jivros. Our race needs her even more than your own, yet I must pretend to be her enemy. I must pretend to be your seductress, and worm from you the knowledge which the Jivros will use to conquer and enslave your planet and your people. I must play this part, unnatural to me, of a cruel and heartless ruler, or they will have me killed by some subtle poison which they will call illness. You see, the Jivros are our doctors. Much of the wisdom of our race is in their hands. They are our priests and our administrators. They leave to us only useless occupations which will not allow us to be dangerous. For centuries they have been taking over every vital function of our life. I am allowed to live only so long as I am a willing tool, and foolish enough to wreak their evil will upon my people. It is a part I cannot continue to play. Every instinct of my being shrinks from what I am forced to order done daily, from what I am forced to allow them to do to human beings."

This was a different kettle of fish than I had expected. This slender, lovely creature, with her hands wrung together in pain and sorrow for her brutally maltreated people, this tear-streaked lovely face contorted with an agony which she had not spoken of to anyone else—this actress supreme, who for all her life had pretended to approve of the alien Jivro's sabotage of her own racial stock—was a heart-rending picture, and her own face told me with its extreme tension that what she said was a fact. But perhaps this alien from space *could* act that well? I preferred to believe her.

"I don't see how you expect me to get a chance to release Cyane of her crystal coffin? I will have no opportunity."

"I will *make* an opportunity. I am not yet alone or helpless, much as the insects would like me to be. This is my only power, that I am the same blood as the people, and not a Jivro. They know that, and constantly try to destroy this strength of mine by making me commit cruelties which I cannot always avoid for fear of such of them as the old Jivro whom you met at the council. So long as I retain his favor, I live. When he raises his finger in the death signal, my days will be few thereafter."

"I think I understand your position. I have heard of puppet rulers before—woman whom I am delighted to learn has a human heart after all. I am wholly with you, and want you to feel that you can trust me to the hilt."

She smiled and dried her eyes. After a moment she leaned forward, and the glory of her beauty, the near nudity of her utterly graceful body struck at me as she fixed my eyes with her own, her face now intent with will to make me completely understand quickly what she knew must be very obscure to me.

"The Jivros fear the power of Cyane, the Croen captive, as they fear death! The Croens have fought to destroy their power for centuries, on many planets in our area of space. Cyane is one of their greatest. She is a scientist of vast wisdom, and one who has developed a technique of increasing the vitality of life within herself, as well as in anyone she chooses to favor. You could well win from her such gifts, if you should release her. It is one reason I wish to release her, in order to win from her that secret of long life which she holds. The Croens are masters of warfare and she would be able, with only a little help, to develop an attack which they could not withstand."

"If they are so powerful, how is it they have not defeated the Jivros?"

"The Jivros are a very ancient, very widespread race. The Croens came into our space-area recently, as time goes, only three centuries by your time. They were lost. There were only a few hundred in a great ship, and they settled upon a small uninhabited and airless satellite of our home planet, were there for many years before they were discovered. When the Jivros attacked them to destroy them, they found in spite of their innumerable ships and countless warriors they could not harm them. But their attacks angered the superior ones, and they began a campaign of extermination against the insect men's empire. Since the Croen were few, they began to recruit from among the Zervs and other groups who were subservient to the Schrees. The Schrees were the ancient tools of the Jivros, and have always held positions as tributary rulers, since the insect-men themselves found subject peoples obeyed the Schrees more readily. They have always kept the priest-like power and, by poisoning and other devices, remove any Schree puppet who displeases them."

"Go on," I said huskily, her rapt face and intent manner, her utterly lovely ivory body, glittering everywhere with the shining powder which she used, the subtle penetrative scent of her—I was hard put to concentrate upon her words.

"I plan to have the crystal pillar opened, perhaps, have Cyane brought to my own chambers, and I will pretend to set up apparatus to read her sleeping mind and so learn from her. Naturally the Jivros will become suspicious of me if I do so, as they fear the knowledge of the Croen which has always proved too great for them. There will be but a few days time between my action in bringing her here, and my own death or her confiscation by the Jivros. But in order to overrule me in this, they will have to make a pretext, charge me with infidelity, convince the old Jivro that I intend harm to him and his. During that time you must find a way to release Cyane and escape with her."

"Why don't you yourself release her and escape with her?" I asked.

"Because I can be useful to her when she attacks us. Besides, I am constantly under the Jivro eyes, and they know me so well they would see my perturbation, they would know something was wrong and forestall me. You alone could do it, and, too, I depend upon your alien knowledge to provide a barrier or two to their overcoming you. Your weapons which you bore when we captured you—do they fear them?"

"I never shot any of them; I don't know."

"Perhaps I will send you with the party to get Cyane. That way you can find a chance to inject the stimulant when they are not looking. They must remove the crystal from about her to move her; it is too heavy to carry otherwise. Then when she awakes, you can find a way to divert their pursuit, provide a false trail. Do you understand?"

"I could try, but I cannot tell if I could outwit them or not."

"They are really very stupid things, the Jivros. Like an insect, their patterns are fixed and repetitive. They are almost incapable of original thought. Once you know them, you can always outwit them. With you will go my brother, Genner. He may be successful where you are not."

"It is agreed then." I stood up; this low couch made my knees stiff. She took my movement as a dismissal of her, and flushed deeply. I smiled at her embarrassment, and went down on one knee to bring my face level with hers where she half reclined on the bench-like lounge.

"Dear lady," I said in English, not finding the necessary Schree words in my artificial memory for a term of respect— then in Schree phrases, "I will do my utter best to help you and your people. It is my duty to my own race, too, as it is yours to yours. Trust me, so far as good-will may go. Together, we will rid ourselves of these unclean Jivros of yours!"

She rose then, and I stood too, still holding her hand that I had seized in my own to impress her with my sincerity. For an instant she looked at our two hands clasped together, then she placed an arm on my shoulder, leaning against me and trembling slightly with emotion. Tears sprang out in her eyes. She brushed them aside.

I did not know what to do. For fear of offending her, I restrained the impulse to take her in my arms, and it took great willpower.

Something about her aroused my deepest admiration. Here was a woman who had been playing a difficult part for years, whose heart was sore with sorrow for her blighted people, and who must yet seem to approve. The signs of long strain were very plain on her face. I understood that this was one of her greatest fears, that her mind would give way and betray her true emotions to the Jivros.

Clumsily I patted her bare shoulder. For an instant her wet cheek was pressed against my own, then she went gliding swiftly away, her face once again proud and empty of all human feeling. At the door she turned, swept her palm once over her face, removing the tears and as the hand passed upward she smiled as sweetly as a young girl, with a pathetic and utterly charming mischievous expression. Then the palm passed downward, and her face was left again stiff and masklike, the lips twisted a little into a cruel thinness, her eyes hard as agates on my own. She was superb, and I silently applauded. Then she was gone.

As I stood there, musing on the nature and the strange life of Wananda, a mocking, sultry laugh made me whirl, for I had thought I was alone.

Standing beside the tall, open window—a window I had examined and found impossible of exit because beneath it was a straight drop of some seventy or eighty feet—was my erstwhile companion and prisoner, the Zoorph, Carna!

Still in her hand was the long, fantastically ornamented drape behind which she had been concealed during my "secret" interview with the puppet queen.

"You!" I exploded. "Where did you come from and what did you hear?"

"Very interesting things, friend Keele. She is a fascinating woman, is she not?" Carna made a pretty mouth, as if kissing something, and with her fingers a gesture new to me, but one unmistakable in meaning. "She now has your simple heart in her hand, to do with as she wishes. You are a fine fool, you!"

"I thought you had psychic powers. You claim to read minds and foretell the future, and you do not understand that she is fine and honest and utterly admirable! You are the fool, Carna!"

She laughed.

"You are right, and not so simple. I said that only to know if your perceptions were keen enough to know that what she said was true."

"Now you know. How did you get here, what do you want, what have they done to you?"

She snapped her fingers, and gave the Zerv equivalent of "pouf."

"They gave me their tongue, as they did you, I notice. They questioned me much longer than you, as they thought I knew the Zervs might be caught. I did not tell them much. But it was my fault that poor Holaf was caught. I did know he was going to try to revive the Croen captive. They wrung that out of me, and then put me in a room directly above this one. I knew that you were below me from the talk of the guards. I made a rope from the hangings and slipped down to see you. I may go back up when I get ready."

She came toward me as she spoke, her hips undulating exquisitely, that sultry smile of completely improper intent on her beautiful face. She wore still the silkily gleaming black net in which I had first met her. It was torn now and even more revealing.

I fixed my eyes on the wide web of linked emeralds at her throat to keep my eyes from hers, for she had a disturbing power to make a man's head swim and his will disappear. It was perhaps no greater power than many another woman possesses, but to me she was particularly devastating. I moved back as she came toward me, smiling a little, and said in spite of my liking for her:

"Keep away from me, Zoorph! You will destroy my soul!"

She laughed huskily.

"What is a soul or so to the passion that could burn us, my Carl? Do you really fear me, stranger from a strange people? Don't you know how much I thirst to drink of your lips! Look at me, you coward. Are you afraid of a woman? Don't you know how curious I am as to how you of this planet make love? I who am a student of love, am most curious about you. Stand still. Here we are prisoners, about to die, perhaps, and you refuse me one sup of pleasure before we die? You are a cruel, and a spineless creature. I despise you, and yet I want you very much."

I kept backing away, around the room, and she pursued me at arm's length, her long graceful legs dramatically striding, making of her pursuit a humorous burlesque, yet I knew she was quite serious about it. If little Nokomee had not warned me against her, I might have succumbed then and there, for, as she said—"What good is a tomorrow that may never exist for us?"

"What did you come for, Carna? To make a fool of me?"

"I thought we might try to escape again, but this pretty queen of the accursed Schrees has charmed you to her will, and I must await a better opportunity. But that does not prevent me from trying to outdo her attraction for you. Do you love her already, Carl?"

"Of course not, I just met her."

This was utterly ridiculous, yet it was a lot of fun and I could see no real reason why I should resist Carna's advances. To me she was about the most attractive woman I had ever met, and I might never see her again. I gave up my retreat, seized the girl almost roughly in my arms, bent her back with a savage, long-drawn kiss and embrace. Then I released her, to see what she would make of an earthman's kiss.

She stood for an instant, her hand pressed to her lips, her eyes wide with surprise, one hand raised as if to push me away. Then she giggled like a young girl, and put both hands on my shoulders.

"So that is what you call love, strange one? Shall I show you how we of far-off Calmar do the first steps of courtship?"

"That would be interesting," I said huskily, my lips burning.

Her voice became low and penetrating.

"You will be two, yet alone, above the all." She said other words whose meanings I did not know. My head swam, my soul seemed to be floating in a sea of new and strange emotions. I sank into a dream state, and with her low suggestive words in my ears, a new world came gradually into form about us, we were two lovers walking among plumed fern-trees, beside deliciously tinkling streams, the songs of birds rang like little bells all about. I was conscious of her warm lips upon my own and of her eyes like two deep dark pools in which my own gaze swam and sank and rose.

Suddenly a rude, loud voice broke in, the dream of paradise vanished from about us.

Before us stood Genner, his face angry, and in the wall I saw the panel by which he had entered where I had thought was only blank wall. He cried:

"You, Zoorph, I had thought not to interfere. But you are not going to enslave this man to your will. We need him, and your people need him too, and what you do is not right, for you know as well as I that if he falls entirely under your spell he will be left no will of his own!"

Carna, not even abashed at the intrusion, almost spit as she angrily retorted:

"What is the difference whose will he obeys so long as it is what we all desire that gets accomplished? He would be better off with my experienced direction than with his own ignorance of our ways, in anything you plan. Do you think I want to be left out? Do you think I do not desire freedom from the Jivros, too? Do you think I want to be made into a mindless thing when I fail to please them?"

"Never mind; get back where you came from. This man is our ally, not our slave, and your behavior is bad. I will hold this against you. Go!" He pointed at the window with one rigid, outstretched arm, and Carna moved slowly away, saying:

"No, Prince, do not think me an enemy! It is only that my heart *is* moved toward this strange one, I wanted him *very* much, and how else can a Zoorph love than as she has been taught?"

The prince smiled at her words, his arm fell to his side.

"Very well, little temptress. Kiss your love goodbye. It may be a long time before I let you see him again. If he desires it, you may meet later on. But I will warn him, so that he does not become your slave."

"I would not rob him of his self, my Prince. I have an affection for this one!"

"We will see that you do not, sweet Carna. Now get out, and be quick. The time approaches."

She darted to my side, where I sat still bewildered by the eerie yet utterly delightful experience with the witchery of a Zoorph, pressed burning lips to my own, caressed my cheek with her fingertips, gave my hand a quite American squeeze. Then I watched her slender legs swing up and out of sight as she went up her improvised ladder hand over hand. She was athletic as a dancer.

"Whew," I said, passing my hand over my heated face, and grinning at the Prince.

"Yes, whew! If it had not been for me you would have become her property, for they are very accomplished in making people do what they want."

"Hypnotism, developed beyond anything I ever heard of! It must be hereditary, such power!" I mused aloud. Genner answered as if I spoke to him.

"The word hypnotism I know not, I guess you mean what we call Zoorph. It is a cult, teaching the art of enslaving others to your will. But she is a good girl, and her Zoorph qualities are not evil. For your own sake, remember always to hold yourself in check, or she will automatically become your mistress. A man does not like to be a slave even to so charming a mistress."

I did not say anything. I saw nothing wrong with the idea just then.

"Were you there behind the panel while your sister and I talked?" I asked.

"Of course. To make sure nothing went amiss. If some curious Jivro had come to the door, she would have joined me in the passage."

The Prince sat down across from me on a low stool.

"I will lead this group she will send to bring the Croen. You will naturally accompany us, as I am to keep an eye on you. Wananda will give you the fluid to inject into her veins. You must not be seen making the injection. Somewhere along the way she will revive. She is an extremely strong creature, and will immediately make her escape. I will order none to shoot at her with vibro guns, as we do not wish her harmed. We will hurry back to get ships to pursue and capture her. But we will be unable to capture her.

"If you can manage to keep up with her in her flight, do so. You should be able to outrun a Jivro; they are not very fast. But whether you can keep up with the Croen, that I doubt. However, make the attempt, and when you are alone with her, explain why we want her to escape, who her friends are. If you do not do that, she may elect to make her way through the wilderness, which would be fatal for her. Knowing she has allies among us, she will find a way to attack us."

I grunted. I did not see how they expected one lone woman, however fantastically gifted with wits and know-how, to overcome the ships, armament and organization of the Jivros, even with Wananda working to neutralize their power.

"She must be a wizard; you expect such wonders of her!"

"There will be a ship waiting to pick her up as soon as she is out of sight of the Jivros who will accompany us. I have sent it already. It waits in the hills by the barrier. With you along, you can contact the remaining Zervs. They will augment your power. I can send more ships manned with my men, later. We have been preparing for this a long time."

"Aren't you doing a lot of talking? Walls have ears, you know, and those Jivros of yours look pretty shifty to me."

"It is the hour of their sleep. They are creatures of regularity, like ants, you know. They live by routine. There are only guards awake. I know exactly where every one of them stands at this moment, where every one of them sleeps. I have not been inactive."

We filed out of the city gate, a party of nearly fifty, a score of them bearers of a big palanquin-like vehicle in which they proposed to carry the Croen's inert body.

I was remembering the brief examination of her that I had made when I entered the cavern of the golden statue.

A four-armed female of near-human aspect, but with a single horn on her forehead. A member of a race from distant space, alien even to these visitors to earth. She had been utterly different from anything I had even imagined as human—yet somewhere, somehow the origin of that race had been similar to our own. I wondered if space was peopled with such near-human races, all descendant from some ancient space-traveling race who had colonized—then passed on into forgotten time?

The party wound on, taking that same trail by which I had entered the cavern with Hank and Jake and Frans. Silently I blessed the fate that had spared me the things that had been done to them. Their only release, I imagined, could be death.

Overhead the rocky walls began to close, the light grew dim, ahead came that eerie glow from the magnetic statue. The prince's eyes caught mine in a swift, silent order to be ready, and the two of us drew ahead of the column. In my jacket pocket I held the hypodermic, one of Schree design, different from a modern medical hypodermic only in that it was decorated with incut figures of glorified Jivros, carved in the crystalline cylinder, and the metal was of gold.

There were only two of the repellent insect-men with us. I surmised they were there only as observers, but that was not the case. They were there because they had to be. I could see an unusual agitation on their blank, bulge-eyed faces, if those insect masks could be called faces. They were afraid of this Croen female, even in her inert condition.

The tall, graceful Schree warriors followed us into the cavern, and last of all came the two hopping Jivros. The intense attraction of the statue drew me, but I remembered how I had avoided it before, and kept my eyes averted. Like light on a moth's eyes, the power of it seemed to strike into the will only when the eyes were upon it.

We gathered around the column of crystal. The Schrees attached a loop of rope to the top, pulled it carefully from the base. When it was stretched out horizontal upon the floor, the two Jivros set to work with little spinning metal disk-saws, cutting a line entirely around it lengthwise. Then they tapped it with small hammers, and the cut cracked through. Lifting off the top section like the lid of a sarcophagus, the Croen lay exposed to the light of day.

I stood entranced by the exquisite beauty and majesty of the naked creature until Prince Genner nudged me with an elbow. Even as he did so, he whirled, pointed, cried out:

"There, through that doorway, one of the traitorous Zervs spies upon us. Catch him, my warriors, before they bring the others down upon us!"

As if drilled or awaiting this order, the tall Schrees set off as one man, running through the same doorway by which I had followed the angry Nokomee.

The prince and I were left alone with the two Jivros, who stood beside the nude figure of the alien Croen. They eyed us, their eyes jerking nervously from our faces to the body of the Croen. Quite calmly the Prince tugged a vibro-gun, very like the weapon Holaf had worn at his waist, from his belt and trained it upon the two horrors.

"This day will come for all the Jivros," cried the prince in a triumphant voice, and shot a terrible blue bolt of force into the body of each of them. The second had snapped a little weapon from his breast, hidden in the folds of his white robe, and as he fell, the beam of it cut a long smoking channel in the floor rock. The prince calmly picked it up, pressed the trigger lever, handed the thing to me. I pocketed it, then stepped over to the nude body of the Croen. I inserted the needle carefully in the artery at her inner elbow, pushed the plunger slowly home, my eyes on her face with a deep awe.

The prince bent beside me, watching her face intently, and both of us stood rapt, waiting for I knew not what except that it would be more marvelous to meet such a god-like creature as this face to face than anything else that had ever happened to me.

But a sound of feet up the corridor made Prince Genner spring to his feet.

"Quick, man, help me get these dead horrors out of sight! I do not trust all those warriors, though most of them are in sympathy with us."

We sprang to the dead things. I bent and picked one up by the shoulders. Surprisingly, frighteningly light they were, as if filled with cotton. Their limbs were truly skeletal, and curiously I tugged the white robe from the strange insect body as I followed the prince. The thorax, the wasp-waist, the long pendulous abdomen, the atrophied center limbs folded across the wasp-waist—the whole thing was like a great white wasp without wings. As we flung them into an empty chamber, I turned the burden face down, and on the back were two thin wisps of residual wings. Once these things had been winged!

We sped back to the side of the sleeping Croen.

I stopped ten feet from the giant figure, surprise, awe, a thrill of admiration filling me! She was sitting up, her hands at her temples, peering about with her great eyes distracted. On her face, even in this condition of tension, still unaware of her surroundings, was the greatest evidence of intelligence I had ever sensed. This Croen race, I realized, was something truly beyond an earthman's understanding.

But the prince had no time for the awed, stupefied condition into which sight of her had struck me.

"Come, Cyane, great one, we have released you, but you must flee at once. I know how weak you must be, but if you can, please rise and flee. This man will accompany you. He is alien to us, and it is better that he be out of the hands of the Jivros as quickly as possible. Go, dear one, swiftly, swiftly—we will find you later!"

The great body moved, gathered itself, stood tottering, gazing wildly about. The prince pointed at the cavern entrance where our footprints still showed in the dust. To me he cried: "Go up the rocky side as far as you can when you reach the slopes. The north side, earthman. Keep going, and conceal yourselves in the bush. I will guide the search away from you."

I ran ahead of the tottering figure and she followed, her steps gathering strength. Faster she followed until we raced along the dim cavern way. The rocky roof opened out and the blue sky showed overhead. The prince had gestured to me when we had entered to a ledge that angled upward from the gully, and I knew now what he had meant.

I could not keep up with the great strides of the now fully aroused Croen goddess. She turned back, picked me up like a child, and in great leaps bounded up the side of the canyon along the ledge. Up and up and over, and still she ran, untiring. I was not rescuing, I was being rescued!

As we ran beneath the shadow of the trees, a figure rose suddenly up before us. I was astounded to see it was Holaf, whom I had thought the Jivros had already dealt with.

"I await you, Cyane, great one, to guide you to safety. The prince has sent me," he cried.

The great striding creature slowed, spoke to me with a voice full of a deep music.

"Do you trust this man?"

"He may be trusted in this case. He has already risked his life to set you free."

She set me down. I looked at Holaf, who was too excited to be amused.

"Hasten, we must get under cover at once. A place awaits, and many men, arms, tools. We have long fought for this day, Cyane!" Holaf was wholly ecstatic to see the success of his plans. I realized the prince had made an ally of him with the same kind of interview the queen had granted me.

Holaf led us around the side of the mountain, keeping in the shelter of the trees, and by a back route to the same hideaway in the mountainside where I had first met him.

I greeted Nokomee with a glad smile, but her smile was not so glad and my heart was hurt to find she was angry with me. But the great Croen creature left us no time for argument.

The caves where the two hundred or so Zervs had hidden for so long were quite numerous and confusingly branched. There was room there to hide an army if needed.

I went at once to the small chamber where Nokomee had placed the packs and camping equipment from the horses, and took out one of Hank's big old forty-fives, belted it on. The old-fashioned belt was filled with cartridges. I also took my own Winchester Model .70. I had a plentiful supply of 130-grain Spitzer-point bullets, a high-velocity, long-range killer that I might get a chance to use. I filled my pockets with cartridges, took a knapsack and filled that. So, burdened down with lethal equipment, I hurried back to Cyane's side. I didn't want to miss a move of that visitor from far space. I wanted to learn, and I had an idea she would show plenty of science if she got into action. The prince wasn't gambling on her for nothing, not with that glorious sister of his in jeopardy.

She had seated herself on that same big bench where I had first met the Zoorph, Carna, and the Zervs were coming and going to her rapidly-given orders. A dozen of the older Zervs were assembling apparatus under her direction, and if I expected to learn something, I saw I was going to be disappointed, for the stuff was inexplicable to me.

I went on outside to the ledge from which the city could be seen. I was worried about how Genner had explained to the Jivros the death of the two who had accompanied him. I had taken a pair of small binoculars from my packs, and seeing activity near the gates of the wall, I trained the lenses upon the wall.

I gave a cry which brought the Zervs speeding to me. I handed the focused glasses to Holaf, pointed at the gates. He put them to his eyes, then he too gave a cry of warning, and raced back to the Croen.

For, filing out of the gates and spreading out across the valley was the vanguard of an army. The glass had shown the streets filled with marching men.

For a few minutes I could not understand exactly what had happened, then I guessed. The prince had asked for permission to use the entire forces of the city in a search for the Croen! The strategy of the man was exquisite. He was playing on the Jivro fear of the Croen to get the military power fully in his hands!

Even as the great limbs of the Croen woman brought her to my side, as I handed her the glasses, round disk ships began to rise from the center of the city one after the other until at least five score of the smaller type were in the sky. After them came two of the larger craft that I knew were really space ships with huge inner chambers in the bottom where the small craft nested.

An all-out search for the Croen was on in earnest!

But now quite suddenly an astonishing thing happened. One of the great mother ships swung in a circle, came alongside the other, and from the great center bulge of the upper surface a blue beam lashed out, struck the other in a slicing flare and sheared off the entire upper bulge in one blow. The great ship faltered for an instant, then began to fall. It struck the ground near the wall with a blinding explosion. As the great mushroom of white smoke began to lift up, the stem of the mushroom blew away, and where the ship had fallen was only a hole, surrounded by bits of shattered metal. The wall near the explosion was breached in a fifty-foot-wide break, and the bodies of men could be seen through the breach, killed by concussion.

From the city a blazing yellow beam lanced here and there in pursuit of the traitor disk, but it darted like a dragonfly, up, down, and zig-zag. The pursuing beam came nowhere near it. Somehow I knew the prince, and perhaps Wananda too, were in that ship, and my heart was in my throat as I thought of the queen in that ship, being shot at by the repulsive insect men.

The army deploying on the plain kept right on marching, columns slanting outward from the center, forming three columns that spread out like the extending prongs of a trident. I could make nothing of it.

Several dogfights had broken out among the smaller disk ships since the fall of the mother disk, but these were quickly over, and the flight came on, swift as arrows.

The remaining mother disk settled to earth on the level land directly below our hiding place, and the smaller disk settled now around it. The army marched on, nearer and nearer.

I looked at Holaf, handed him the glasses.

"I don't know whether we are lost, or, whether the prince has joined us, deserting the Jivros in the city you Zervs built."

"None but Prince Genner knew our hiding place, and who else would place themselves under our fire range, knowing we were here?" Even as he spoke, the door opened in the side of the great disk, and the prince sprang out, turning to assist his sister to the ground.

The Croen, Cyane, standing beside me, suddenly leaped off the ledge, her long limbs making easy going of the sloping detritus below. Seconds later she was running easily across the plain toward the ship, and I was surprised to see the prince and the queen bow their knees to her, kneel before her as if praying to a goddess. She touched the bowed heads with her fingertips, and the three figures then entered the disk and the door closed. The ship lifted, took off alone in a southerly direction, flying higher and higher and out of sight. Even as it disappeared, another great disk lifted from the city, set out in the same direction in pursuit.

But the smaller ships below lifted at once as they sighted this pursuit, set out after the second mother disk.

"I guess we're going to miss the fighting," I said to Holaf.

"We can get into it when the time is right. We've got to move at once. The Jivros know our location now. Come on!"

Holaf strode back into the cavern that had been the Zerv's hideout for so long. I followed, stopping curiously to examine the apparatus which the Croen had abandoned on the advent of the prince. It was a kind of still, bubbling now with a wick lamp under the red fluid, and nearly a gallon of the end product had collected in a big jar.

"What was this distillation all about?" I asked Holaf.

"It was a medicine she was making for the Shinro. She said that an injection into their blood would increase their perceptions to a human range of intelligence, and that then we could use their resulting rage against their mutilators. It is only a temporary effect. It will wear off in a day, leave them again to the stupidity the Jivros gave them. Now, she's gone, I don't even know the dosage. It is useless, the prince took her from us."

"We can use it, if it is complete. I have the needle I used to revive the Croen. Bring the stuff; we'll try it."

"We could circle the army, get into the city…" said Holaf, his eyes glittering on mine.

"Let's go," I cried, getting his idea.

We were near a hundred and fifty young Zerv fighters, and perhaps as many women and old men and children. We wound through the passages of the tunnels in the mountain, came out on the far side from the valley. Along the mountainside we traveled, and I realized we were at the mercy of any force we met, being too few and too hampered with baggage and the helpless members of the Zerv families.

But Holaf knew what to do. He pointed out a trail toward the wilderness to the thin little column, told them where to take cover and await his return. Then with myself and a dozen of his best warriors, he turned his face again toward the Jivro stronghold.

We circled the valley, marching hard, crossing the upper narrow end. Coming toward the city, twilight was closing down, and we made the last few miles in complete darkness.

Near the walls, Holaf chopped a thirty-foot sapling, which we carried to the wall. A young Zerv swarmed up the pole, let down a rope to help the ascent of the others. I climbed the rough pole after him. I hadn't the athletic ability of these Zervs who seemed to like to climb ropes hand over hand. So over and down into the silent city we went, drawing up pole and rope after us, hiding them in the shadows of the wall.

Like shadows we stole along the streets, and after long minutes heard the unmistakable feet of the Shinros. They came with that ghastly mechanical rhythmic tread, eyes staring, backs burdened. I guessed that now their burdens were materials for the defense of the wall. We followed, and not far distant from the breach of the explosion of the disk ship, found our chance. They were accompanied by four of the hopping Jivros, and upon the back of each a young Zerv sprang, silent as stalking cats, striking them down, crushing their skulls with vibro-gun barrels.

Holaf and I set to work immediately on the mindless Shinros, injecting shots of the red fluid into their veins one by one, varying the shots to gauge the effect. But it was potent stuff, and before I had the third man under the needle, the first was speaking in a hoarse, angry voice.

"What has happened to me, what—what?"

Holaf said: "These are almost all graft jobs, were once captives and normal men. The result, if this shot works, is going to be a thoroughly angry man, fighting mad for the blood of the Jivros." Then he raised his voice to the newly revived Shinro.

"You were made into a beast of burden by the Jivro insects! Tonight you will get your revenge. This shot of sense we are giving you will last only till daylight, so your life does not matter—it will revert to the beast in the morning. Go and spend your time where it will hurt the Jivros most— spill their blood. Their power is ending this night! This is the beginning of the end for all the Jivro parasites of our race. What we begin tonight will not stop till every Jivro in the ancient Schree group of planets is dead and gone!"

As we completed our injections, the column stood waiting, but a column of sane men, ready to shed Jivro blood for their revenge.

"Go as if to get more burdens of stone to repair the wall. When the Jivros show themselves, kill, get weapons, do not stop killing until they are gone or you are dead. You have but this night; make the most of it."

The column plodded off, in the same apparent condition we had first met them. But in their brains was boiling, enraged sanity, in a condition of complete rebellion, of murderous intent.

"They'll sell their lives for something worthwhile, tonight," said Holaf into my ear, as we set off on their trail. We intended to make the most of any opening the revived Shinros made for us.

Two more columns of toiling Shinros we liberated with injections, then our supply of fluid was exhausted. Just what more to do to hurt the Jivros we didn't know.

"How many ships do those Jivros have? Why are they always in hiding? Since I've been around here I haven't seen a dozen of 'em at one time!" I asked Holaf, my feet tired from sneaking along the deserted streets.

"They never come out in the open except for some express reason, such as driving the Shinros to work. They still have probably a score of ships."

"Twenty of those big disks?" I asked.

"Yes, I would say that many. But they will not bring them out to battle unless there is no other way. A Jivro never does anything he can get a human to do. Now that they have only the Shinros in the city, with the army out there searching for the Croen—and maybe the most of it deserting to some rendezvous the prince sent them word about—they will do nothing unless they must. You know how a spider hides when it senses danger?"

"There are many insects that hide when they are in fear."

"They have that trait, but they also have courage when desperation drives them. Now they are holed up in their strongholds, waiting developments. They will only come out to fight if they see an opportunity to crush their opposition, or if they are driven forth."

Suddenly the long beam of a searchlight lanced across the night sky above, then another and another. For an instant a huge disk showed in the beam. It tilted and drove abruptly sideways out of the light. The beam danced after. It was not seen again, and still more beams winked on, began to search, systematically quartering the sky.

"I would say our friends, the Jivros, were in for it. The prince and the Croen are attacking," I said to Holaf.

He grunted.

"I didn't expect it so soon. They do not have the strength in ships. But the Croen must have some stunt figured out to equalize their power."

We moved along pretty rapidly, keeping to the shadows, and soon were again at the side of that flat, paved place from which the disk ships took off. Overhead loomed the beetling walls of the palace from which the prince had led his people in revolt—manned now by the Jivros. I wondered how it felt to them to have to do their own fighting.

The beams moving about from the top of the building lit the streets about us with a distinct glow. It was no place to remain. We moved back along the parallel street, and I had an idea. Whatever was I carrying all this weight of heavy game rifle and knapsack of cartridges, and not even getting in position for a shot? I gestured to Holaf and tapped the rifle, pointing up.

He got the idea, led me to a dark doorway and we entered the building, made our way to the roof. Lying prone along the parapet of the roof, I adjusted the sights for two hundred yards, and swung the rifle sight slowly across the flat roof of the palace. The reflections of the big searchlights made the surface quite bright, and about each light was a group of the tall white-robed Jivros. They made perfect targets!

I began to fire, taking my time, centering each figure exactly. At each shot, one Jivro fell. I had fired but a score of times, and the white-robed creatures began to leave the lights, to cluster about the archway over the roof stair.

Grouped as they now were, I did not need to aim. I fired four more clips as rapidly as I could load them. Then the remaining Jivros began to swing the great beams in a frantic search for the deadly fire. As the beam swung toward us, Holaf seized my head, pushed it beneath the parapet. The beam swept on without pausing. I raised my head and kept on firing.

All of the beams but two were now stationary and unattended. I could not reach these, the angle of fire was wrong; but I could see the base of the lights, and as they swung again toward me, I fired into the center of the beam. It blinked out. Holaf clapped me on the shoulder.

"Get the rest of the lights, man, never mind the damned insects! The Croen will take care of them soon enough."

One by one I put out the search beams, the sky overhead grew dark again.

"These are the creatures who expect to conquer the earth!" I cried out scornfully to Holaf. "They could be bested by a bunch of boy scouts with twenty-twos!"

"They have never fought! They are only priests, not warriors. They are not thinking of conquering anything now, without their willing servants. They are fighting only for life!"

Overhead still wheeled the circle of guarding disks, manned, I knew, by the inexperienced priest-like insect men. I took a careful aim at the glowing transparent bulge in the center of the nearest, hoping the alien plastic was as soft as the earth plastics. But there was no way to tell if it had pierced the shell of plastic, or if it had done any harm.

Fumbling in my pockets, I pulled out a loaded clip, lay there pondering with the clip in front of my nose. Absently I noted the black band around the nose of the bullets, indicating it was a high-velocity, armor-piercing cartridge, manufactured by the U.S. Army for exactly such emergencies as I faced. I did not know if it would prove too big a powder-charge for my rifle, I did not know then even how I came to have the cartridges. Polter had bought some Army ammunition and these must have been among his things. I may have been firing them steadily and not known the difference.

I inserted the clip, and lay there with my fore-sight following the disk ship in its steady circling flight. Just where would an armor-piercing steel bullet do the most harm? I shot the clip out at the great round body of the thing, trying to guess where a hit might damage machinery or pierce fuel tanks. There was no visible result, and I gave the flying disks up as a bad job. How did I know they were built to resist meteors in ultra high-speed space flight? It didn't even occur to me.

"Where're your buddies?" I asked Holaf. He lay beside me peering down into the street below.

"Gone to join the Shinro. They are storming the doors of the palace now." He gestured toward the street.

I leaned over the parapet. Below in the street the hideous, mutilated bodies of the Shinro moved in a mass. They had brought up a huge beam, and were pounding it against the great palace doors. Others climbed toward the tall barred windows, some of them slipped through. But of the white-robed Jivros there was now no visible sign.

I was about to send a few shots through those same windows, when a waving white cloth from a window near the top of the huge structure drew my eyes. A sudden fear struck my heart. Could that be my Zoorph, left there—could that be Carna? I felt sure it was, and something warm and pitiful seemed to flutter in my chest as I thought of her alone among those hopping Jivros. I got to my feet, started across the roof.

"Where are you going, earthman?" asked Holaf, placing a hand on my shoulder.

"I am going into that place, but there is no need you accompanying me. I think I saw Carna at her window, a prisoner! I would like to free her."

Holaf gave a cry of unbelief.

"No, you cannot do that! The Croen means to destroy that place down to the ground. Carna will have to perish with it. It is too bad, but you cannot enter there. I know what is going to happen."

Even as he spoke, a great white blossom of flame spurted suddenly over our heads, spread and spread across the sky above the circling ships. Looking up, my eyes were struck blind. I dropped to the roof surface with agony. Then came the terrific, stunning concussion. The prince was letting off the fireworks at last! I exulted, even as I despaired. Somehow I only now realized that this waiting, strange Zoorph in her prison, who faced death because forgotten by her friends—*must not die!* In my heart some warm thing she had waked there with her magic breathed, moved, sprang into complete life. I could not see her die! I must get into that place that I saw was doomed, even as I now saw two of the great ships above falter in flight, turn and slide downward at increasing speed. The concussion had broken them, perhaps destroyed the life within them. I realized that in a short time the same thing was going to happen to the headquarters of the Jivros.

Below, the booming of the great ram against the palace door ceased, there came wild shouts, cheers, running feet, terrible screams of agony. I ran down the ramps up which we had ascended to the roof. Heedless of danger, I raced along the dark street, across the wide-open space surrounding the palace.

About the palace door the dead were sprawled in mangled heaps. Among the dead were several white robes, now stained with the pale blood of the Jivros. I surmised the frightened creatures had opened the door, intending to kill the men wielding the ram—and had been unable to do a complete job. The doors gaped open. I stumbled over the reeking heap of slain. A dying man raised one horrible crab claw to me, called out my name! It was Jake, his ugly face now a horror. I had not even known he had received the reviving shot of the Croen medicine.

I bent to hear his words, but he only looked at me for a second, his lips formed one word: "Gold!" He laughed bitterly, repeated it: "Gold, hell!" and then his head dropped lifeless.

I raced on into the place, and at my heels came Holaf. In his hands he held the vibro gun, and on his face was a wild triumph. He kept crying aloud:

"Death to the Jivros! An end to tyranny!"

I had no time for the political angles which so inspired Holaf. I raced upward along the same paths by which Prince Genner had led me to my own detention quarters. I did not know how to reach Carna's room except that it lay directly above my own. I raced into the open door of the prince's quarters, and to that window by which Carna had entered. I leaned out, shouted at the top of my voice.

"Zoorph, are you there?"

Her voice came to me with a message of relief, yet it justified my worse fears. She was here, and the place was about to be blasted by some titanic explosive of the Croen science creation! Her words were indistinct, but the tone was almost mocking, and I thought I heard her laugh.

"Can you come down, Carna, or do I have to come after you?"

Seconds later the knotted drape she had used before swayed down into sight, I grasped it to steady it. Her bare legs followed, and now her voice came to me with a sweet mockery:

"Never let it be said that Carna required a lover to climb to her window! Rather let it be said that passion made Carna risk…"

Overhead another of the terrible blasts of flame blazed across the sky. The light blazed all about us, and Carna leaped from the window ledge into my arms even as the concussion struck at us. I lost my balance; we fell to the floor together…and her voice went calmly, mockingly on, loud in the sudden ensuing silence:

"…death itself to be at her lover's side! And it sounds as if we both risked death this night!"

I lay there staring into those mysterious depths of her strange wide-spaced eyes, and she giggled a little. I could not help laughing. Even as I struggled to retain sense an almost hysterical laugh of relief broke from me.

We got to our feet, and in spite of the terrible danger, our arms kept hold of each other, our eyes still held together, and our lips were drawn together and burned there for minutes.

"This is madness, woman, we must get out of here. The Croen has made bombs for the prince's ships. He has rebelled against the Jivros, released the Croen, Cyane, they will blast this place, perhaps the whole city, before this night is over!"

"So no one placed any value on the life or the help of Carna but the earth man! Why did you come here for me, Carl?"

"I saw your scarf at the window. I learned then what I did not know before—I could not let you die! Do you know what I felt when I knew you were still in this prison?"

"Of course I know. You see, Carl, the magic of the Zoorphs is really a magic of love. You love me, and I willed it so. You will always love me now!"

I was not entranced by her words.

"We have no time for a discussion of metaphysics or of love, woman. Come, we must get out."

Carna gestured toward the doorway. I whirled, stood frozen with startled nerves. There stood the old Jivro whom I had met in the council beside the queen. In his hands were no weapons, and at his back were no tall Schree guards. I wondered if the desertion of the Jivros had been so complete. Even as I stooped to retrieve the heavy rifle from the floor, his hands gestured, and the rifle eluded my reach, seeming to glide across the floor. I followed it, and he gestured again.

Some force seemed to freeze me. It had not been nerves that held me before, I learned, but his eyes upon me! Unwinking, the ancient master of what worlds unknown to me, regarded me, and I knew I was helpless before the power he controlled. My lips moved, but no sound came out.

A sudden blast of light came from the window, and the vast concussion shook the building terribly. For an instant I felt freedom in my limbs. I tugged out the .45 at my belt, leveled it, fired. The Old One staggered, his eyes blazed at me, and his hand gestured again. The gun fell from my hands, and some terrible black thing struck into my brain, tearing, rending. I fell forward into blackness...

Swirling nothingness, a dry cachination as of some dead-as-dust thing laughing at life itself, a shuddering vibrance flooding through my flesh in waves of terrible nausea, a dim glow that grew and grew into terrifying painful brilliance, then paled and died again into the swirling blankness that was not death, but a knowledge of deep injury...

Again and again the swirling horror of my brain slowed, almost stopped. My eyes almost opened into the painful light, and the deep interior vibrating sensation swelled into overpowering violence. I sank again into darkness. Over and over I struggled almost to the doors of consciousness, only to be shoved back by the consciously controlled exterior force.

At last the sickness passed, and my mind quieted. I struggled into wakefulness. As I opened my eyes, the face of the old Jivro gaped with its noseless, bulging eyes not a foot away, the thin, wide lips and mouth hanging open like a trap, the ridges across the mouth like a fish, white and horrible.

I retched at the repellent sight, and the mouth moved, the words came out so strangely, like a mechanical voice:

"Tell me, earthman, how is the weapon with which you shot my men on the roof made? What are the details of its construction, and the formula for its explosive?"

I almost laughed.

"You are ridiculous, old insect! Such things are known only to technicians in factories, not to mining men like myself."

Again the blinding light struck at me, the sickening shaking of the vibrance welled through me. I sank and was raised again to consciousness.

Still the same foolish old insect face, the same bulging ignorant eyes. The words:

"Tell, then, how this Croen and the forces of Prince Genner may be overcome? Speak, earthman."

The compulsion moved me, and I answered:

"There is no way you can overcome them, Jivro. You are doomed, and there is no hope for your tyranny over the Schrees to continue. They have tired of the Jivros, and you deserve what you are going to get."

Again the sickening application of force and again the exterior compulsion to speak. I said:

"Your only chance to get back power is to get forces from your home in space, wherever that may be. You cannot overcome these fighting men and their weapons, which are as good as your weapons, for you Jivros have relied for too long upon the Schrees and Shinros for your fighting, and for your thinking too, by the questions you ask. Have you not done any thinking in your life, that you ask me such silly questions?"

A change came over the old creature. I knew he was wounded, for I had seen the glistening milky fluid pouring from the wound in his breast. He leaned weakly against the table to which I was strapped, his eyes on mine glazing over with death. The wide lips at the very bottom of the flat face, moved:

"The Jivro Empire is ending, I think, earthman. We dug our own grave when we relegated all unpleasant duties to our conquered races. For an age the Jivro has been a creature shunning all work and effort, even thinking. We were bound to lose our grip. I see now that I am really foolish, and not a strong being of intellect. Our doom is written, and the day of the writing was that day when we conquered and enslaved the Schrees."

"Now you are talking sense, Old One. You see what is plain to all others; at last it becomes clear to you. But you are dying, and it is too late for wisdom to come to the Jivros. Once you set your feet on the path to greatness; but when you did evil, your feet naturally turned to the downward path of decadence. Evil is not a way of life, it is a way of death."

The bulging eyes on mine flickered with a fierce inner fire for an instant, then the head bent lower. For an instant he tottered there beside me, then crashed to the floor with a sound like a bundle of dry sticks.

I turned my head, saw that I was in the chamber of my first interrogation, and the sound of feet about me was the Jivro "doctors," moving to carry away their ruler. I saw the sleek body of Carna on a table but a dozen feet away. Three of the tall white-robed insects bent over her, one moving a control in a great lamp device, another scribbling on a pad, and the third was speaking. Evidently the Zoorph was getting the third degree, too. I lay back weakly. I felt as if I had been through a washing machine and some of my buttons left in the wringer.

As I closed my eyes, a vast *boom* crashed into my ears, the table jumped beneath me, pieces of masonry fell bounding on the floor and I raised my head, staring wildly. Evidently the prince and the Croen were still bombing the place.

I tugged at the straps on my wrists and ankles. They gave a little. I kept on tugging, turning my head as far as I could to see how the insect men were taking their bombardment. They stood, near fifty of them, in a group by the door.

Evidently they had started to run out when the crash came, but had stopped when it was evident the roof was going to remain intact. If those things had any sense they would be in the deepest sub-basement they could find, I figured. The Schrees must have been carrying them as helpless parasites for too many centuries to realize they could do without them, for them to be so inept.

Straining my neck, I watched the grotesque high-breasted white figures about the doorway, they were tittering to each other in some tongue I did not know, a strange sound like the rasping of corn husks under squeaking wagon wheels. Suddenly the whole palace shook terribly, the floor seemed to reel, an unbearable sound raged at my ears. I cringed from the pain of the sound. When I opened my eyes, the whole mass of the Jivro medicals was jammed in the doorway, struggling to get over each other, and the squeaking and rasping increased into a bedlam of sound. I laughed, a deep "ha ha," and from the neighboring table Carna cried:

"See what wonderful creatures are the tyrants when things are not going their way. If I had known they were like that in war, I would have killed them all myself long, long, ago. I would have poisoned them, and when they asked me who did it, I would have said, *boo* and they would all have run away and hid!"

As the last of them got through the door, I gave my loosened straps one mighty pull, and the heavy leather tore. I could hear it part in the sudden silence. Again and again I strained, and at last the leather parted entirely. My right hand was free. Feverishly I tore at the other fastenings. There could be but little time left us before that bombing struck dead center and brought the whole palace down. We had to get out. I knew it quite as well as those fleeing insect men.

Free at last, I rolled off the table, landed on all fours, leaped to Carna's side, and released the buckles of the straps.

As she sat up, her face level with mine, she pursed her lips, and I gave her a hearty smack. As her arms went about my neck, I picked her up, raced through the doorway, along the passage, down the ramps. I was weaponless, but I had no longer any fear of the Jivros. I saw a group of them busy in a big chamber as I passed, but I raced on, spinning around the next corner, down the ramps and on...on...until I felt the coolness of fresh air ahead, ran out beneath the stars again, and along the shadowed street.

Putting my Zoorph back on her feet, we raced toward that breach in the wall. Over our heads the great blasting explosions went on, and I saw but three of the circling disks left to the defense of the city.

Outside the city wall we stopped to catch our breath, leaning against the wall in the shadow.

Carna said, musingly: "It is all over for the ancient Empire of the Jivros, if help does not come for them tonight. For, now that they are seen to be so helpless without their slaves and their fighting men, the news will spread. Planet after planet will rise against them. This is their finish!"

"They expected to conquer earth, Carna. They could never have done it. For a little while, perhaps, but not for long."

"They might have! They are like ants; they have a highly developed pattern of activity. But when that pattern is disrupted, they are lost. They do not think—they remember."

"We've got to make contact with the queen and with Genner and the Croen. We will be left out of things." I was wondering what Carna's future plans were.

"You are interested in the beautiful sister of the Prince?" asked Carna.

"You are interested in the so handsome Prince?" I answered in the same tone of voice.

"Of course, what woman would not be! But I am more interested in you, for I fell in love with you. But I can fall out again, and maybe—who knows…" she laughed.

"What's more to the point, Carna, is she interested in me?"

"I could tell you," said Carna, her eyes mysterious on my own, luminous and huge in the darkness.

"Well, perhaps you had better tell me, then."

"Why? I love you!"

"You mean she *is* interested in me!"

"Very much, and she is a very smart woman who has ways of getting what she wants. I am very much afraid she will take you with her to space when they go, and leave poor Carna in her ruined city, with no one but the wild beasts and the dead bodies. This will be the end of this place."

"You are wrong!" I smiled, thinking the girl was flattering me.

"No, not wrong, dear earthman. I am very much afraid of the future, for I am to lose you, but I have a way of avoiding that."

"And what is that way?"

"You will find out when the time comes, and you may like it very much!"

"Let's get away from this wall where we can see what's going on…"

We plodded across the level, grassy valley floor, walking backward some of the time, watching the great circling ships above the city's center, and the lancing blue paths of their rays stabbing at some darting adversary high above them.

Then from the western sky came a series of round low shapes, speeding so rapidly the eye could hardly distinguish them from the darkly glowing horizon. After their passage, in a close series, came the air-scream of falling missiles, high-pitched, then came a terrific cannonading of explosions.

Fountains of fire sprang up in exact sequence, one after the other. The ground shook and shook underfoot, each shock seeming greater, to add its strength to the one preceding it. I knew that this was for the Jivros the end of their plans on earth.

Simultaneous with the arrow-swift flight, two great blazing lances of blue fire shot downward from the ships far overhead, transfixed the circling spheres one after the other. They tilted, plunged slowly, faster and faster—ended in great splashes of fire and sound somewhere in the city below.

I mopped my face. The night was hot, and relief flooded me.

"We got out of there just in time, Miss Mystic!"

She nodded, her white smile in the night a beautiful thing.

"What is this Miss Mystic word you use?"

"It means Zoorph, Carna. It is U.S.A. speech."

"U.S.A. speech," she parroted. "Some day I will talk U.S.A. speech, too, like you!"

"I hope so. This tongue of yours gives me cramps in the jaws."

We plodded on across the grass, heading for the cliff ledge where we had met. I knew no where else to go.

Quite suddenly came a soft sussuration overhead, a light-beam lanced down, pinning us there. I tossed Carna aside, rolled myself out of the path of light. But mercilessly the light beam spread, until we were again within the circle of illumination.

But no blue death ray followed. The dark shape settled to the earth beside us, and the door in the side opened.

I sprang to my feet in glad surprise to see Holaf in the round doorway, motioning us to enter. He cried:

"Come, the day of the Jivro has ended, there is work now for men to do!"

Carna laughed happily, ran to the doorway, and as Holaf caught her waist and swung her up, she kissed him on the cheek, still laughing in abandoned joy to know that finally the centuries-long nightmare fastened on her people was ended. I followed more sedately, wondering what now? I thought of poor cross-eyed Jake Barto, and of the three fortune-hunters who had gone the same path—and as I shook Holaf's hand, questioned the ecstatic confidence of release upon his face.

"Suppose the Empire sends ships here, will they not destroy all you have gained? Why do you feel so sure their power is broken? They were but few here?"

"They will not send ships, for no messenger got away. What do you think the ships of the prince have been doing? This is the beginning of their end!"

"How did you get out of the palace? The last I saw you, you were storming the place, gun in hand, and cheering…"

"When the bombs began to burst against the very roof, I got out. I killed a few Jivros first, though! It has been a good time; the best of my life!"

"Were you picked up as you picked us up?"

"Of course. Look there who it is that has done us the honor…"

My eyes followed his finger pointing through the far arched doorway to the control room. At the bank of levers and dials, her face intent upon the scene through the circular plastic dome, sat Wananda. Inadvertently my eyes went to Carna's face; she nodded once, vigorously. I knew she meant:

"See, I have told you the truth. She knew where you were, her heart told her, who else would descend to pick you up while the fighting was still going on?"

I went to her, and stood for a moment beside her, watching her swift hands, the light on her midnight hair, the delicate superb chiseling of her forehead and nose, the exquisite aura of womanhood about her—she was every inch a queen.

She turned, startled to find me there, then smiled, and a warm flush spread slowly from her neck upward to her temples. She knew that I knew! She laughed a little quiet sound to herself.

"That is why the Zoorphs are hated, earthman. One can never keep a secret!"

"You must have the powers of Carna yourself, to know that she told me." I answered.

"I have studied their methods. One comes by such talents hereditarily. The Zoorph is only an organization which concentrates on taking in and teaching such gifted children. I, as a princess, had a tutor of their sect. I know that you love her, too, you know."

"And not yourself. But she confesses that I love her only because of her skill at hypnosis, or something of the kind. To me that seems unfair, but I cannot help it. I love her, though I am drawn to you. But why should we concern ourselves with these matters? You will go back to space with your ships to carry rebellion to the other Jivro strongholds. I will be left behind to mourn you both."

"Why should you be left behind? Do you find the Schree or the Zerv company so repellent?"

"Not at all. I should desire nothing more than to see the worlds of other suns, other places in the far paths of space. Yet…"

"Yet what? Have you a wife here, children?"

"No, not that. But I have possessions it cost me many years of effort to acquire."

Carna came silently into the room, stood on the other side of the queen. For an instant Wananda closed her eyes, and some subtle sense of my own told me they were talking with each other in a way I could not hear. Wananda opened her eyes, turned to me, smiling whimsically.

"Carna suggests that she will give your love to me in return for a certain favor."

"Do you want my love, Wananda?" I asked softly.

She did not stop smiling secretly to some sound she heard and I did not.

"You see, earthman, our race has never developed the morals and inhibitions which your people find so necessary. We are polygamous, and not apt to be jealous. She offers to give you to me as a royal husband in return for the privilege of being your slave, your housekeeper, your body-servant as it were. What do you say?"

I was stunned. So openly to be bargained over; frankly to be invited to marriage, to two women at the same time! Weakly I countered:

"Your people would object to an alien consort!"

"The word is strange to me. Among us you would be a ruler if you married me. Among us all men have several wives. But women have but one husband."

"You are offering me the rule of the Schrees?"

"Yes, and if our coming war with the Jivro creatures turns out well, it will mean not one planet, but many. I cannot say how many, as some of those never allied with the Schrees before will naturally gravitate to us in gratitude for our releasing them from the Jivros. I am agreeable mainly because I know that we need your earth science, your different culture—as wedded to our own science we would be invincible. We will need everything finally to conquer the ancient ingrown tyranny of the Jivros. I am not offering you exactly any bed of roses. Besides, I like and trust Carna. I can understand why she loves you, and why she bargains for any part of you. She knows I have but to exert my own wisdom of Zoorph to release you from her hold on you."

"I see. Let me get this straight. You love me; it is agreeable to you that I continue to love Carna; but I will love you too. Two wives who love me, a kingdom, and the chance of knocking over a whole empire of insects who have parasitized human races in space and meant to do it here. There is no way I can refuse!"

Carna laughed.

"With two of us working your mind for you, how could you refuse?"

Wananda frowned at Carna's frankness.

"It is stated in the nineteenth law of Zoorph code that no victim is ever to be told of his enslavement openly, Carna. Why do you break the law?"

"I don't know, Wananda Highest. I think it is because I want to be fair to him, and give him a chance to do his own thinking, too."

I grinned.

"Our race has long been familiar with your so-called magic, dear ones. We call it hypnotism, and if you think I cannot resist it, remember that I shot the Old One with his eyes upon me."

Wananda suddenly set the big lever she held into a notch, turned to me, her face full of a charming surprise which I yet knew was an act.

"So you think you can resist your wives' wills, do you, earthman? Come, Carna, let us humble his boasts once and, for all!"

Their two lovely faces pressed cheek to cheek, the two pair of eyes bored into my own, and four quick slim hands gestured about my chin. A dizzy enervation swam into me as though I were bleeding to death, as though honey and whiskey were being poured down my throat, as though I had fallen suddenly onto a pink cloud of spun candy.

Visions of terrific pleasure began to hum in my head, my knees gradually gave way beneath me, until I was on my knees before the two women. My hands were unconsciously extended as if to fend them off, and each of them seized a hand, pulled me to the round bench at the back of the control cabin. They stroked my cheeks, began to murmur their "magical" phrases in their mysterious mystic secret words, and my wits began to float into a very genuine paradise where their two faces, side by side, became flower and fruit and tree and earth itself.

When I awoke from the dream into which they had sent me, Carna was seated beside me, nodding sleepily, her head on her chest, and Wananda had returned to the controls of the ship. As I looked at each of them, I found *a new something had been added*! I loved each of them equally well!

I sat up, stretching. Sometimes it is comforting to have problems decided for one. Now I did not have to go through any excruciating pangs of conscience or guilt or fight myself into a state of not wanting one or the other of them. They had just adjusted me to the situation mentally, and I felt that everything was perfect in the best of all possible marriages for me!

"Well, I'm getting hungry!" I cried, apropos of nothing except that I did feel pangs.

My Zoorph did not even get up. She reached out one hand to where a covered tray sat on the bench beside her, and handed it to me. I took off the lid, and on it were broiled chops, steaming deliciously baked beans, some kind of soft brown bread—fruit, a sweet perfumed wine.

"The master is hungry, Carna will provide!"

If I get cross-eyed as Jake Barto, it will be from trying to see two women at once.

Oh yes, I forgot to tell you that Nokomee became the prince's third wife. I wished her happiness. For me, two are enough!

THE END

If you've enjoyed this book, you will not want to miss these terrific titles...

ARMCHAIR SCI-FI, FANTASY, & HORROR DOUBLE NOVELS, $12.95 *each*

D-1   **THE GALAXY RAIDERS** by William P. McGivern
SPACE STATION #1 by Frank Belknap Long

D-2   **THE PROGRAMMED PEOPLE** by Jack Sharkey
SLAVES OF THE CRYSTAL BRAIN by William Carter Sawtelle

D-3   **YOU'RE ALL ALONE** by Fritz Leiber
THE LIQUID MAN by Bernard C. Gilford

D-4   **CITADEL OF THE STAR LORDS** by Edmund Hamilton
VOYAGE TO ETERNITY by Milton Lesser

D-5   **IRON MEN OF VENUS** by Don Wilcox
THE MAN WITH ABSOLUTE MOTION by Noel Loomis

D-6   **WHO SOWS THE WIND...** by Rog Phillips
THE PUZZLE PLANET by Robert A. W. Lowndes

D-7   **PLANET OF DREAD** by Murray Leinster
TWICE UPON A TIME by Charles L. Fontenay

D-8   **THE TERROR OUT OF SPACE** by Dwight V. Swain
QUEST OF THE GOLDEN APE by Ivar Jorgensen and Adam Chase

D-9   **SECRET OF MARRACOTT DEEP** by Henry Slesar
PAWN OF THE BLACK FLEET by Mark Clifton.

D-10   **BEYOND THE RINGS OF SATURN** by Robert Moore Williams
A MAN OBSESSED by Alan E. Nourse

ARMCHAIR SCIENCE FICTION CLASSICS, $12.95 each

C-1   **THE GREEN MAN**
by Harold M. Sherman

C-2   **A TRACE OF MEMORY**
By Keith Laumer

C-3   **INTO PLUTONIAN DEPTHS**
by Stanton A. Coblentz

ARMCHAIR MASTERS OF SCIENCE FICTION SERIES, $16.95 each

M-1   **MASTERS OF SCIENCE FICTION, Vol. One**
Bryce Walton—"Dark of the Moon" and other tales

M-2   **MASTERS OF SCIENCE FICTION, Vol. Two**
Jerome Bixby: "One Way Street" and other tales